Schaefer, Laura
The Teashop Girls

DATE DUE

PRINTED IN U.S.A.

The Teashop Girls

The Teashop

Girls

illustrated by
SUJEAN
RIM

LAURA SCHAEFER

A Paula Wiseman Book
SIMON & SCHUSTER BOOKS FOR YOUNG READERS
New York   London   Toronto   Sydney

SIMON & SCHUSTER BOOKS FOR YOUNG READERS
An imprint of Simon & Schuster Children's Publishing Division
1230 Avenue of the Americas, New York, New York 10020

Book design by Jessica Sonkin
The text for this book is set in Venetian 301BT
The illustrations for this book are rendered in pen and ink
Manufactured in the United States of America
2 4 6 8 10 9 7 5 3 1
Library of Congress Cataloging-in-Publication Data
Schaefer, Laura.
The Teashop Girls / Laura Schaefer ; [illustrated by Sujean Rim].—
1st ed.
p. cm.
"A Paula Wiseman Book."
Summary: Thirteen-year-old Annie, along with her two best friends, tries desperately to save her grandmother's beloved, old-fashioned teashop in Madison, Wisconsin, while she also learns to accept the inevitability of change in life. Includes proverbs, quotations, and brief stories about tea, as well as recipes.
ISBN-13: 978-1-4169-6793-4 (hardcover)
ISBN-10: 1-4169-6793-1 (hardcover)
[1. Tea—Fiction. 2. Tearooms—Fiction. 3. Grandmothers—Fiction.
4. Best friends—Fiction. 5. Friendship—Fiction. 6. Business enterprises—Fiction.
7. Madison (Wis.)—Fiction.] I. Rim, Sujean, ill.
II. Title. III. Title: Tea Shop Girls.
PZ7.S33232Te 2008
[Fic]—dc22
2008036158

To Karen Meyer

and

everyone at Imperial Garden restaurant
in Middleton, Wisconsin

Acknowledgments

I'd like to thank my parents, Linda and Michael Artz and Michael Schaefer, for their ongoing support and encouragement. I also want to thank all of my grandparents, my brother, David, and my extended family for cheering me on.

Thank you to my tireless and talented literary agent, Stephen Barbara, and my truly extraordinary editor, Alexandra Penfold, who saw promise in my ideas and made this book come to life. Thank you to my real-life Teashop Girls, Aimee Tritt and Nicole Soper. Finally, a big thanks to all the witty people in my life whose lines I "borrow."

The Perfect Cup of Tea

Instructions by Annie Green

- Bring fresh cold water to a rolling boil,
  but don't let it boil for too long.
- Let it come off the boil and settle down for a
  moment.
- Pour water into a teapot containing a heaping
  tablespoon of your favorite loose tea leaves.
- Let the leaves bloom and steep for at least three
  minutes.
- Pour the tea into your favorite preheated cup.
- Sip and smile.

Chapter One

"My dear if you could give me a cup of tea to clear my muddle of a head I should better understand your affairs."
—CHARLES DICKENS, *MRS. LIRRIPER'S LEGACY*

There's a right way and a wrong way to do many things, and when it comes to tea, my opinion is one should not mess around. My grandmother Louisa first taught me to brew a fine pot of tea when I was five years old. She told me what a nice job I had done, and I announced I wanted to be just like her when I grew up. Louisa laughed merrily at the time. I hoped she wouldn't laugh today. I couldn't bear the thought of being laughed at today, which is why I, Annie Green, am hiding out in the storage room of the Steeping Leaf.

Well, not *hiding* exactly. That would be silly. I love the

Leaf, and there isn't anything out there to hide from, least of all my grandmother Louisa. But the fact of the matter is I am here in her teashop, she doesn't know it yet, and the reason for all my sneaking around is I need to psych myself up for what I am about to do.

You know how some people have weird/cool talents, like being able to wiggle their ears back and forth just by concentrating really hard? Well, I have one too. I can stand on my head forever. Like, seriously forever. My two brothers can even try to tickle my feet to knock me over, and I just make faces at them, upside down, secure in the knowledge that I am just as steady on my head as they are on their feet. Which isn't, come to think of it, as steady as, say, *Louisa* is on her feet, but it's pretty darn good. And as a bonus, when I stand on my head, I can feel myself getting smarter and calmer. I think it has something to do with the fact that a headstand is a real yoga pose.

With two younger brothers and an older sister, it's hard to ever find even half a moment alone. And the silence of the storage room is blissful. It's just me, upside down and Zenlike amidst a few dozen boxes of loose tea, some old teacups Louisa hasn't taken to St. Vinny's yet, and my "Perfect Cup of Tea Instructions," which I've written on a whiteboard that, for readability's sake, has also assumed the sirsha-asana pose.

I am almost ready to ask for a job here as a barista. And when I do, I will be calm, centered, grown-up, and only *slightly* red in the face. I am a tiny bit worried because sometimes my family doesn't take me seriously. Everyone else in my family already has their "thing"—Beth is all "college, college, college . . . did I mention that I'm going away to college in the fall?" and Luke and Billy have the lock on the local emergency room—skateboarders, it's like they have a death wish or something. My mom has her students, and my dad has his engineering projects. And I have tea.

Okay, I'll admit, I'm interested in a lot of things and I tend to announce my newest obsessions rather frequently—but working at the Leaf is not just a phase. I've always loved the Leaf and confess that I consider it partly, well, mine. Am I ready to be a barista, taking money, making complex foamy drinks, and asking after the customers' families like the perfect hostess? I think so. I hope Louisa does, too.

Still staring at the board and mentally picturing each and every step of brewing a pot of tea, I sighed happily and closed my eyes to fully commune with the delicious smells of the shop. Inhale. Exhale. "I am one with the tea. The tea is one with me. I am one with the t—"

The storage door banged and there was some

commotion. My eyes snapped open, but all I could see was a pair of legs in jeans. And a box. A really big box. A really big box coming straight at me. "Hey, watch out!"

Instead of changing course however, the startled jeans-wearer swung the box around. Right into me. "AUGHH!" he cried, tripping a little and juggling the box. It was definitely a *he*, I thought as I tumbled over, directly into a precarious stack of napkins, tea samples, and the shelf with the old cups. *CRASH!* went one cup. Then, *CRASH! CRASH! CRASH!* came three more. Ouch.

The napkins flew everywhere, and some of the samples burst open, sending leaves and particles of rosehips, chamomile, orange spice, and white tea every which way. I stared at the intruder from the corner where I was sprawled out, confused. I thought Louisa was the only one who ever came in here. Well, and me, of course. *CRASH!* One more cup slid to the ground.

The intruder set his box down *veeery* slowly and righted the shelf I had tipped. I was just about to sputter something extremely non-Zenlike when the words got tangled up in my tongue. My scowl fully retreated as my eyes widened. Why hadn't I seen him before? It occurred to me that most girls could go a whole *lifetime* of seeing strange boys in teashops (grocery stores, movie theaters, stadiums . . . you get the idea) and not lay eyes on someone so perfectly gorgeous.

"What were you *doing*?" he asked, offering me a hand up. I took it slowly, my stomach flipping.

"I . . . I . . ." Apparently, I could no longer speak. Great.

He cocked his head expectantly. I stared. And stared. And stared. Finally I said the first and best thing that came to mind. "I was standing on my head. I do that."

I do that. Wow. Smooth. I could feel my face reddening.

"Oh." He looked at me as if I were some amusing— yet potentially deranged—creature from another planet. "Why?"

I didn't get the chance to reply because the door to the main shop opened again and Louisa came hurrying into the room, her scarves flowing luxuriantly behind her.

"What on earth? Is everything all right? Annie, my sweetness! What are you doing here?"

Just when you think your face can't get any redder, know this:

It can.

Chapter Two

Tea gives you courage.

—ANNIE'S GRANDMOTHER LOUISA

Nothing had gone according to plan. How was I supposed to ask for a job *now*, with tea leaves poking out of my already crazy hair?

Louisa helped me to my feet and dusted some tea leaves off my shirt. "Jonathan, this is my granddaughter Annie. Annie, Jonathan," She acted as if my destroying half of her storeroom was perfectly normal.

"Jonathan's grandmother is an old friend of mine from the ashram. She studied in India at the same time I did . . . gosh, that must've been over thirty years ago now. Where does the time go? Anyway, he's been helping me out with some of the inventory." I remembered to shake hands firmly and even managed to—sort of—look him in the eye as I wheezed out a "Nice to meet you."

"Hey, Annie." Jonathan nodded, grinning openly at the entertaining spectacle that was yours truly. I began straightening the room, and he pitched in to help. Louisa looked at me bemusedly. I knew she was waiting for an explanation, but I wasn't ready to tell her the real reason I had snuck in through the back of the shop.

"I just wanted to see if the new delivery had anything interesting . . ."

Louisa nodded tactfully, smiled, and hooked her arm in mine. "Well, in that case," she said as she led me back toward the shop. I glanced behind and watched as Jonathan gathered the rest of the teacup shards and took them outside to the trash. As he moved out the door and out of sight, it was like a fog had been lifted. I plopped down on my favorite well-worn stool at the counter and took in the whole scene. Everything was pretty much how I left it the last time I visited. The furniture was old but funky—funky in a good way, not funky in an "it bothers my nose" way. Lively music played, and the shelves were packed with every variety of tea and coffee you could imagine. Green, scarlet, black, vanilla, rooibos, Earl Grey, Darjeeling . . . you get the idea.

People were scattered inside of the shop, reading

papers and chatting. There was an old man at one table holding an enormous book called—I think—*Ulysses,* and a group of ladies at another table exchanging pictures and recipes. I smiled. I've been coming here for a *very* long time, sometimes with my two best friends, Genna and Zoe, who live nearby. Louisa nicknamed us the Teashop Girls. Ever since we were six years old, she has helped us with our Tea Handbook, a tea-centric scrapbook filled with cool recipes and quotes and old advertisements. It is my most treasured possession.

"So how *are* you, my dearest darling? Look!" Louisa led me behind the counter of her store. "We have a new variety of black tea in today," she said as she plucked a glass jar off the shelf, her armful of silver bracelets clinking musically. Louisa opened it and waved it before my nose. I closed my eyes and inhaled deeply. I could almost taste blackberries. And something else . . . maybe cinnamon?

"Mmm. That smells delicious." I reached for my favorite teapot, the white porcelain one with a curved spout and hand-painted blue flowers. It reminded me of the lilac bush out on the Steeping Leaf patio. Louisa smiled and took our cups off the shelf, then scooped some of the new tea into the pot so it could bloom in the hot water. We grinned at each other as the good smell wafted about. Louisa fussed a bit with one of her scarves, sending it fluttering behind her shoulder. Her crystal earrings twinkled in the afternoon light. I'm sure coolness skips a generation because my mom, with her sensible khaki mom-pants and cardigan sweaters, is kind of boring-looking next to her mother. There might still be hope for me, as long as I spend a *lot* more time here at the shop.

"How was school today, my lovely?" Louisa tucked a piece of my wild hair behind my ear and pulled out a lingering tea leaf as we both waited for our tea to fully steep.

"Pretty good," I replied, remembering my day. "My least favorite person, Zach— you probably remember him, he's come in here to bother us—finally got in trouble for being in the hall when we were supposed to be learning about the Etruscans." I smiled a little, warming up. "Then they did a locker check and discovered he had three Milios subs in there from, like, nine years ago, which is what was smelling up our entire floor. Ew. Anyway, everyone in my grade is excited for summer and hardly paying attention to the teachers at all, so we had a pop quiz in math and I was totally freaked out that I completely failed, but somehow miraculously did awesome on it." I stopped to catch my breath. "How is *your* day going?"

"Quite, quite well. There's the new tea, of course, and

when I was doing my tai chi this morning, I saw a mother robin tending to her nest on our rafters. I'll show you." Louisa winked at me and pointed out the window to the corner of the roofline. Sure enough, a clump of sticks and brush was tucked safely behind the gutter. I smiled.

"I wonder how long she's been there." We watched the nest for a few moments, hoping to see some tiny new beaks. One of the best parts about living in Madison is how completely nature is a part of the city. Sure, there are the obvious ways, like all its lakes. But it's also the little things, like people's prairie gardens in place of lawns and flowering roundabouts in the middle of the neighborhoods' intersections. Louisa and I *highly* approve.

"Only a day or two, I think." Louisa checked our steeping tea; she was a master at gauging just the right moment to remove the leaves. "Mmm, smells like perfection." Louisa poured our cups, her scarves never even coming close to getting in the way. It was, like, against the laws of physics or something. I added a little sugar to mine and took a big sip.

"This is delicious. But I actually came down for another reason . . ." This was it. Now or never. I set my cup down and hesitated, my pulse quickening. I hoped my little storeroom episode wouldn't give my grandmother reason to hesitate when I asked to be a real barista. "So, um . . . Louisa, I've, uh, been thinking, and I'd really, really, really like to work for you here in the shop. I know I'm a bit young, but you don't have to pay me much, and I promise I'll see to everything you need. I . . . I practically know this place better . . . better than my own bedroom, and, and . . ."

Louisa put her hand lightly on my shoulder and I stopped stammering and looked at her anxiously.

"Annie, dear, what a surprise!" She paused and smiled. "It would be a joy to have you here more often, but do you really want to start working? Childhood goes so fast, love."

I cringed at the word "childhood." This was not going well. Thirteen—almost fourteen—was hardly childhood. Besides, I had helped Louisa lots of times before. It would be so easy and fun to do it regularly, like an actual grown-up.

"Louisa, I've thought about it a ton, and I know I am ready. I love your shop more than anything, and I've wanted to work here for a long time. You can count on me."

"I know I can, dear."

"I made a whole list for you. I am always on time, and I *think* I have good chi, and some of your customers know me already . . ." I gave Louisa my "Reasons to Hire Your Favorite Grandchild" list.

Reasons to Hire Your Favorite Grandchild, Annie Green

1. I take showers with seven different organic gels, shampoos, masks, beads, conditioners, and skin cleansers and therefore smell good all the time without hurting the environment.

2. I think my chi is in good order. I mean, I hope so.

3. Old people like me because I know who Jimmy Stewart and Bea Arthur are.

4. I love tea and adore coffee. ~~Which, according to my dad, is why I will never grow taller than 5'1".~~

5. I am extremely punctual, and am, in fact, often early as I have nothing better to do besides study or go to the mall, which is a shrine to mindless consumerism and should be avoided at all costs unless Hollister is having a sale.

6. I am awed by the long history and endless health benefits of tea. And I know that orange pekoe has to do with the size of the tea leaf, not the color or flavor. Weird.

7. I am very cheerful. Annoyingly so, say my brothers, the grandchildren who, I believe, did

not write thank-you notes after receiving lovely birthday presents. I think we can both agree the two of them aren't the best judges of character. I have the perfect level of cheer for barista-hood.

8. The Tea Handbook is full to bursting . . . so I must know more about the Way of Tea than practically anyone.

Louisa chuckled as she read it over.

"This is some list, Annie. Did you talk to your parents about this?" she asked gently.

"Yes, and *Mom* even said it was okay." You would not believe what I had to go through to get my parents to agree to allow me to try to get a job. I knew my mom would cave eventually; she loves the Leaf almost as much as I do. The shop has been around *forever*, even when my mom was my age. I didn't mention how my mom had said she'd like to see Louisa taking it easier. Louisa was vibrant, but she was nearing *seventy*. Meanwhile, I was bursting with energy.

"You sound very serious, Annie. I respect that." Louisa nodded carefully. I could feel myself holding my breath. I let it out sharply as I prepared to further build my case. I could see a couple of the customers staring at me. Was it just my imagination, or had people stopped chatting?

"Thank you. I would like to come in a few afternoons after school, and maybe one full shift on the weekends." I looked my grandmother right in the eye. She smiled at me, bemused. There was a long pause. I wondered if I should talk some more or forget the whole thing and tell her I was just kidding.

"All right then, dear, consider yourself hired." Louisa's eyes sparkled as she watched my grin widen. She pulled me into a big bear hug.

"Really?" I asked, breaking away from her hug. "Really, really?"

"Really," she replied.

I clapped my hands and looked around the shop through new eyes, feeling proprietary. My first workplace. A girl just couldn't ask for a better one.

"Let us toast!" Louisa laughed as she refreshed our cups. We clinked our china and sipped the tasty brew. I set my cup down, still bursting with excitement. I decided to do a little victory dance—a cross between a spastic sprinkler and the Charleston, I think.

I could feel the eyes of many a shop patron fixed on my impromptu celebratory hopping, but I didn't care one bit.

"So, my dancing queen, when would you like to start?" Louisa asked me.

"Today? Tomorrow? I don't know . . . soon!" I kept jumping happily from foot to foot.

As the words left my mouth, I heard something behind me. It sounded like muffled snickering. I shimmied around and saw Jonathan come out of the back room. How could I have forgotten he was here?! I abruptly stopped moving, midhop, as my face reignited. I smoothed my hair a bit and cleared my throat, trying to look normal. The one thing I have going for me is memorable hair. But it only looks okay when it is under house arrest by various products such as gel, styling cream, mousse, etc. Which I had not bothered with today as Beth was hogging the bathroom. Curly red hair is the pits. Curly red hair when your face is blushing is the double pits. Maybe triple. Jonathan looked at me and smiled, opening his mouth as if to say something and then closing it before any words came out. Why, why, *why* did he have to come out in the middle of the celebratory Sprinkler Hop?

"Wonderful news, Jonathan! I've just this minute hired Annie as our newest barista," Louisa explained.

"Cool. Welcome." He moved to a chair and started paging through a notebook. His long legs barely fit under the table, and his dark blond hair hung in his eyes. I waited for some crack about not letting me in the storage room, but I guess older boys are too mature for that sort of thing.

"Come in tomorrow at eleven, dear, and I'll show you the register," Louisa said to me over her shoulder. I wondered if *he* would be working. I couldn't take my eyes off him; thank goodness Louisa was on her way to her office and pretended not to notice.

I surveyed the Leaf once again. It had been a pretty good day as days go. Got job, check. Met extremely cute boy, unexpected, but check anyway. Completely embarrassed self in front of grandmother, teashop patrons, and aforementioned extremely cute boy, check, check, check.

As I was carefully placing my cup in the sink, something *very* strange happened. The music abruptly stopped playing and the cozy interior of the Leaf went dark.

This is an ad Louisa gave me. It's from the 1940s and shows how many people used to consider tea a summer drink. Louisa explained to me how, when she was a kid, no one had air-conditioning in their houses. So they would sit on their porches with cool beverages like iced tea and visit with neighbors. I think this is the reason Louisa barely ever uses her air-conditioning at home. She would rather be outside with her friends and a cool drink, just like the lady in the advertisement.

Chapter Three

"I can just imagine myself sitting down at the head of the table and pouring out the tea," said Anne, shutting her eyes ecstatically, "and asking Diana if she takes sugar. I know she doesn't but of course I'll ask her just as if I didn't know."
—LUCY MAUD MONTGOMERY, *ANNE OF GREEN GABLES*

So, did Barista Boy say 'welcome,' like, with an eyebrow thing, or just 'welcome' like Mr. Nelson when we show up late for social studies?" Genna was the master of guy-versation, especially since she discovered the Relationship section at the University Bookstore. Zoe, Genna, and I were sprawled out on the floor of my room, having a miniparty to celebrate my official entrance into the working world. We made guacamole and biscotti, an odd combo, I admit, but always a crowd pleaser. With Genna flinging her arms around, some of it was sure to land on my rug or bedspread. It would not be the first time.

"Um, somewhere in between?" I answered her kind of halfheartedly. I had a fairly massive homework assignment to finish and my parents said my grades had to "impress them" if I wanted to work at the shop. But Genna could talk voice tone for hours. She wanted to become either an actress or an artist, which meant that she liked to dissect human—mostly boy—behavior a *lot*. Her name was actually Jenny, but she changed it when we were in the sixth grade and insisted on the *g* spelling because she thought it was more "cinematic." I still can't believe all the parents and teachers we know are okay with this.

I was so happy to see both Gen and Zo, but the fact that the lights went out in the Leaf was nagging at me. Right after it happened, Louisa sent Jonathan home and closed early for the day. The look on my grandmother's face worried me. Something was really not right. I kept remembering how my mom said the shop wasn't busy enough lately and how she was concerned Louisa wasn't paying all the bills promptly. My stomach knotted up a little when I thought about it.

"The important thing is that she *got a job*, okay? Not that some high school boy said 'welcome.'" Zoe was lying in the middle of my floor, perfectly straight. She is half Indian, and her amazing, shiny, perfectly smooth straight hair, which I'm totally not one bit jealous of, was cascading around her. Unlike Genna, with her constant wild gesturing, Zoe conserved her movements. She was an athlete and pretty much unflappable. Zo usually wore almost all white; she had this ability to *never* spill anything on herself. If more than 30 percent of a conversation drifted to the topic of boys, she got annoyed. "If my parents let me have a job I'd want to work at the Leaf."

Zoe raised her straight legs four inches off the floor. I stayed where I was, draped over the director's chair stolen from my brothers' bedroom.

"Thank you, Zo."

The last time we all managed to hang out outside of school was a week ago, when we went to the Memorial Union terrace, by the university union. And by hang out I mean I hid under an umbrella most of the time, coated in SPF 175, while Genna and Zoe ran around with a Frisbee and some boys from our class. Okay, I'll admit it, I felt left out, and as sunny as it was, the extreme measures to prevent further frecklege was a little bit of an excuse. As you might have noticed, I get kind of shy around boys, not sure what to say. We'd all been friends for so long—since kindergarten, when Genna taught Zoe and me to braid hair—but the thing is, I still look and feel mostly like a kid, and my friends are starting to seem like actual, I don't know . . . women. It's weird.

Really weird. The fact that we were all in my room talking about my new job and my new crush was heaven.

"So, how is Louisa?" Genna asked. She scratched at the fake tattoo on her lower back.

"The same; she's good," I replied.

"You remember how she always called us the Teashop Girls when we were in elementary school?" Genna asked. I grinned.

"Of course I remember." *She still does*, I added to myself.

"You were the president!" Genna said, whirling around and pointing her finger at me. Zoe laughed.

"And you were the life-long queen."

"We were awesome back then." Zoe nodded. "We were the princesses of the Steeping Leaf kingdom."

"That's right. While all the other kids were eating PBJs, *we* were making scones." Genna arched her eyebrow. I giggled. "Hey, whatever happened to the Handbook? I want to read the rules again."

"Umm . . . the ones we wrote in third grade?" I hesitated. I wasn't sure it was a good idea to tell my friends how carefully I had saved them after we stopped talking about our little club. Even though Gen and Zo didn't add to the Handbook anymore, I still worked on it quite a bit. Suddenly I felt a little embarrassed.

"Come on, you remember," Zoe said. "No boys allowed at tea . . ."

"I have them right here," I confessed. I dug in my messy closet for a few moments and unearthed a big purple box filled with treasures. Right on top was the Tea Handbook itself. Among the recipes, advertisements, and snapshots of us were several colorful copies of the TSG rules written in Zoe's precise penmanship. It was more perfect than any other nine-year-old's writing, that was for sure. I grinned and did a little curtsy as I presented them.

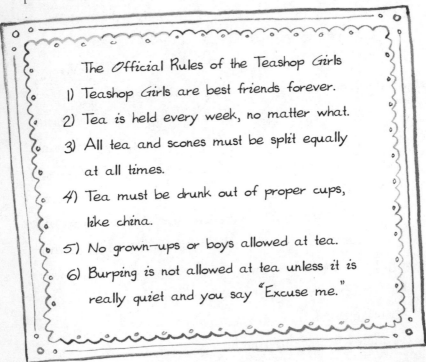

The *Official* Rules of the Teashop Girls

1) Teashop Girls are best friends forever.

2) Tea is held every week, no matter what.

3) All tea and scones must be split equally at all times.

4) Tea must be drunk out of proper cups, like china.

5) No grown-ups or boys allowed at tea.

6) Burping is not allowed at tea unless it is really quiet and you say "Excuse me."

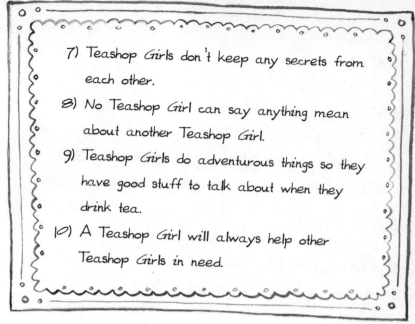

7) Teashop Girls don't keep any secrets from each other.

8) No Teashop Girl can say anything mean about another Teashop Girl.

9) Teashop Girls do adventurous things so they have good stuff to talk about when they drink tea.

10) A Teashop Girl will always help other Teashop Girls in need.

"I forgot how hilarious these were! I want a copy," Genna demanded.

"These are pretty good for a bunch of third graders," Zoe agreed.

I wondered why we no longer followed the Rules. When had we abandoned the weekly tea ritual? Zoe and Genna huddled around the Handbook, laughing and reminiscing. Would my friends care as much as I did about what was going on at my grandmother's shop? We had already stopped having tea together. They were so busy with theater and tennis and things. These were two people who were actually *ready* for high school and all the stuff that came with it. Unlike me.

"So the lights went out when I was in the Leaf," I finally blurted out, trying to sound more casual than I felt. I tapped a stack of books with my foot, which promptly fell right over and made a huge mess.

"What?" Genna and Zoe both turned to me.

"Off, off? Or just, like, flickered?" Genna asked.

"Off, off," I replied. "No lights, no music, no power at all!"

"It must have been a mistake," said Zoe.

"That's what I thought at first, too," I said. "Stuff happens. But I think there might have been an unpaid bill. Louisa says that the Steeping Leaf doesn't have a hip crowd; it has a hip-replacement crowd. What if they've mostly all croaked, and there're no new customers?"

Zoe's eyes got wide, and Genna looked worried. The chip Genna had been eating fell to the floor, forgotten. Both of them stared at me, as if I'd just said we had to repeat the eighth grade.

"Confession." Genna paused as she searched for the right words. "I was on the Leaf's block a few days ago . . . but I went into that new place across the street . . . for a whipped-cream espresso thingy." She looked ashamed and didn't say anything for a moment, which was unusual. "I feel soooo horrible, I swear I'll never do it again. We *must* go in there more."

"Yes," Zoe said. She was still holding the years-old Teashop Girls manifesto. "We've got to do something."

"We definitely do," I said, relieved that Gen and Zo seemed as bugged as me. Well, a little bit relieved. "I'm worried about the Leaf's bills. There has got to be a way to get people to love the teashop as much as I—as *we* do."

All three of us nodded.

Maybe

A Taoist story
as told by Annie Green

Many ages ago there was an old farmer whose horse ran away. When his friendly neighbors heard the news they said, "What bad luck!"

"Maybe," said the farmer. He was a pretty calm guy, like my dad.

The next day the farmer's lost horse returned and brought with him three wild horses. To that the neighbors said, "How wonderful."

"Maybe," said the old farmer.

The following morning his son tried to ride one of the wild horses and broke his leg when he was thrown off. Again the neighbors said, "What bad luck."

"Maybe," said the old farmer.

The very next day the army came to the village and drafted all the young men to fight. They passed over the farmer's son because of his broken leg. Once more the neighbors congratulated the old man on his luck.

"Maybe," said the farmer.

Chapter Four

If you are cold, tea will warm you. If you are too heated,
it will cool you. If you are depressed, it will cheer you.
If you are excited, it will calm you.

—WILLIAM GLADSTONE, 1865

Genna stayed behind with me after Zoe went
home. Zoe and her family always ate dinner at
precisely the same time—her stepdad was a
retired navy officer and liked things to be on a schedule.
Her house was the cleanest I've ever seen in my life. Zoe
and her younger brother probably had to, like, vacuum
under their beds and present their fingernails for inspec-
tion. I knew she missed her real dad a lot. He moved back
to Mumbai after her parents split up, and now she sees
him only once a year. Genna's family was different. She
was an only child and pretty much got to do whatever
she wanted. Her parents were in the south of France for

the weekend, so she was home alone again with her dog, Barley, and her housekeeper, Sarah.

Gen gets lonely sometimes—even with her five million cable channels—so I always tell her she can hang out here whenever she wants. Our townhouse is anything but lonely. My family consists of two parents, four kids, and three pets (five if you count the fish, which I don't). It is never, ever, quiet or peaceful here. I'm not really sure how I ever *think* with my two brothers slamming into walls. I brought home chamomile tea from the Steeping Leaf once to try to calm everyone down, but so far it has done nothing except put my dad to sleep in his recliner. My little brothers, thank goodness, are now addicted to Guitar Hero. It actually brings the decibel level *down* about half a notch, if you can believe that.

"Did Zo tell you that Zach Anderson made the tennis team? They're going to have to scrimmage," Genna said as she puttered with my nail polish collection.

"Ugh, I don't want to hear about Zach," I said. "Poor Zo."

Zach Anderson was the type of boy who would pour warm Red Bull on a young plant. He'd been a sworn enemy of the Teashop Girls since kindergarten. There are even pictures of him and his annoying friends spying on us on the school playground in our elementary school yearbook. (Obviously, they were terrible spies.)

"He's kind of cute lately," Genna said. She had started talking to Zach and his rich, snotty friends a bit in home-room. Seriously, does she not remember when we were all in fifth grade and he put the cockroach in my desk?

"You are beyond disgusting."

"I know." Genna refused to acknowledge the rather large stack of schoolbooks I had pulled out and was try-ing to organize. I always forgot that when I invited Gen to hang out at my house I never got anything produc-tive done. It was like this one time when we were nine and Louisa asked me to help her reorganize and dust all the Leaf's bookshelves. Much to my grandmother's delight, I brought Gen and Zo with me. But while Zoe and I carefully wiped and alphabetized, Genna sprawled out on one of the Leaf's comfy couches and continually squealed out beauty tips from the first book she had picked up: *Leaves of the Goddess*. It had pretty much always been like that, since the three of us had become friends. Zoe and I were Genna's guaranteed audience. But to be fair, it *was* a Friday and I *am* a freak for even thinking about homework on a Friday. "So how are you going to make Jonathan fall in love with you?"

"You mean my mere presence won't be enough?"

"A strategy never hurt."

"I'll just try to do my job well, I guess. You know, talk

to him and stuff." I shrugged and blushed a little.

"Just *think* about accidentally getting locked in the storage room with him, okay? I'll help." Guerrilla tactics, Genna's favorite. "Hey, Jonathan, Annie needs some help with stock in the back. Click." Genna smiled devilishly.

The thing is, even if I *was* locked in a storage room with Jonathan—and not causing a calamity with an ill-advised yoga pose—I wouldn't know what to do anyway. I had never really kissed anyone—Daniel Hansen in the seventh grade *did not* count. I am terrified I'll totally mess it up. Everyone else at my school seems so experienced, and I'm not even sure where noses go. I quickly ran through my very short list of romantic encounters.

1. Danced with Jake Chang twice in sixth grade. If you call swaying at arm's length dancing.

2. Went to a movie with Kenny White because the school colors are green and white and everyone thought we should go out. His mom took us. We hardly talked the whole time and avoided eye contact at school for, like, a month after.

3. Sort of kissed Daniel Hansen at Genna's pool party last summer. Someone dared him to. He mostly missed my mouth, thereby kissing only a very small section of my chin. After that,

*I jumped in the pool and contemplated not
surfacing for several hours. My lungs betrayed
me and I had to come up. Stupid lungs.*

I wasn't like Genna. Her latest drama was with a freshman named Josh from her theater group, who refused to accept that Genna wanted to break up with him. He called and texted her tiny pink cell about ten times a day. Just in case you were curious, I don't have a cell phone, tiny, pink or otherwise, because my mom says I am too young. Sigh.

Zoe hangs out with this nice guy named Peter who plays soccer and lives two blocks over. I wasn't even sure if Zo liked Peter *that* way, but it was a good system for both of them because they always had someone to play basketball with and no harassment from the gossips at our middle school. Whenever Genna bugged Zoe for make-out tips, Zoe just looked at her like she's crazy and changed the subject. Zoe doesn't have time for romantic problems. She's a genius, as far as I can tell. Her mother and stepfather give her enough to worry about. They expect Zo to, like, win the French Open or a Nobel Prize, preferably both. I guess it's the high-pressure approach. Thank God my mom and dad are at least somewhat normal. Genna and I sometimes feel bad for Zoe and worry about her. Since she's on her parents' regimented academic-and-athletic-full-ride-to-Harvard track, Gen and I end up hanging out without her a lot of the time.

"So you wanna get Beth to take us to Shorewood so we can go spy on Zach? I think his bedroom's on the first floor."

"Gen!"

"What?" All innocence, of course.

"Focus, Genna. Focus. What we really need to do is figure out how to get more people into my grandmother's shop." I hated to interrupt Gen when she was in boy mode, but some things were just more important.

"You're right. You're totally right. I promise I'll think about it and come up with something great. I love the Leaf." She looked serious, even grabbing the Handbook and hugging it to her chest. I decided we needed some tea to inspire us, so we wandered down to the kitchen. I filled up the stovetop kettle and pulled two mugs out of the cupboard.

Genna paged through the Handbook and her face lit up with happy nostalgia. It made me glad to see her remember all of her own contributions to the book. I knew that she understood how important it was to help the Leaf now. We clinked our teacups together and it felt just like old times. I smiled; we would do whatever it took.

Mom's Gingerbread Cupcake with Lemon Cream Cheese Frosting

INGREDIENTS

4 tablespoons unsalted butter, softened

⅓ cup white sugar

⅓ cup molasses

1 egg

1 cup all-purpose flour

1 teaspoon ground ginger

1 teaspoon crystallized ginger, finely chopped

1 teaspoon ground cinnamon

½ teaspoon ground allspice

½ teaspoon ground nutmeg

¼ teaspoon salt

1 teaspoon baking soda

⅓ cup milk

8 ounces cream cheese

¼ cup half-and-half

1½ teaspoons lemon zest, finely grated

2 cups powdered sugar

Preheat the oven to 350 degrees F. Line a muffin tin with paper liners. In a large bowl combine the butter with white sugar. Add the molasses and the egg to the creamed mixture.

In another bowl stir the flour, two kinds of ginger, cinnamon, allspice, nutmeg, and salt together. Dissolve the baking soda in the milk. Add the flour mixture to the creamed mixture and stir until combined. Add in the milk mixture. Pour the batter evenly into the lined tin.

Bake at 350 degrees F for 20–25 minutes. Allow to cool.

To make frosting: combine cream cheese, half-and-half, lemon zest, and powdered sugar. Frost cupcakes once they are cool.

Makes 10-12 cupcakes.

Chapter Five

You can't get a cup of tea large enough or
a book long enough to suit me.
—C. S. LEWIS

D o we have any more oranges?"

My dad peered into the stuffed refrigerator and tossed three to my mom, who actually caught them. "Thanks." She abandoned a mushy kiwi and pressed the citrus into the ancient juicer, humming a lively cantata. My mom is a professor of music theory at the university. She can play just about any instrument and has perfect pitch, but my brothers' obsession with Guitar Hero aside, her musical talents rubbed off on exactly zero percent of her kids. We are all practically tone deaf. Or at least we claim to be to avoid piano lessons. In any case, she's apparently a pretty big deal. And she seems to know it, too. As far as I can tell, our household is a dictatorship and she's the beloved despot. It pretty much works, though.

"Annie Banannie!" Dad called out in a voice that was way too sunshiny for a Saturday morning. I cringed; I really wished he wouldn't call me Annie Banannie anymore.

"I made you an extra pancake, Annie Banannie. Can't send you to your first day of work hungry," he said as he passed me a heaping plate.

"Dad, really. I'm not a lumberjack." I grimaced at him and passed two of the cakes to Billy, who promptly started repeating "Annie Banannie" at me over and over because he knew just how much I loved it. I scrunched my nose at him.

"Don't break Grandma's teashop, Annie Banannie!" Luke chimed in obnoxiously. "Like the time you busted my PlayStation," he added, pouting. For the record I did *not* break anything. He didn't even know what he was talking about. For one, she prefers to be called Louisa, and for two, a person cannot "break" a shop.

"Eat up," Dad encouraged as I scowled at the boys. He grinned at me and replaced the pancakes I had passed off. I gave up and started eating. There was no way I was going to admit to my rowdy family that my stomach was flipping around at the thought of being at the Steeping

Leaf all day long with the cutest boy barista in the known universe. I'd never, ever hear the end of it. Genna was bad enough. Last night on the phone after we discussed potential strategies for a Teashop Action Plan—more on that later—she had insisted on reading *Rescuing the Sinking Ship of Your Relationship* out loud for five straight minutes. Never mind that I didn't *have* a relationship to rescue.

"Annie, what's with your upper lip?" Beth looked up from her volume of Rilke long enough to stare at me inquisitively. I instantly dropped my fork to cover my mouth.

"Um, I put on an exfoliating mask and left it on too long." This was not true at all. I had noticed a slight fuzz on my upper lip and tried my mom's decade-old depilatory cream on it. It got rid of the fuzz all right, but it also made all the property between my nose and lips look like a candied apple. I had almost forgotten about it until my ever-charming older sister was nice enough to remind me. *What a nightmare.* I had to start work with a red-skin mustache. *Why? Why? Why?*

"Billy! Slow down. Share with your brother." My mom simultaneously wiped Billy's face with a napkin and poured Luke some juice. The two boys were getting syrup everywhere, which was typical. Beth glanced at them fearfully. She sat on a high stool, trying to look sophisticated above the cacophony (love that word, I think it was probably invented just for us Greens). Mom's food went untouched as she shooed Molly, our retriever, away from the table and made sure Beth got the gluten-free pancakes from the separate pan. Everyone talked all at once about the weekend.

"Okay, I've put your chore lists on the whiteboard," my mom announced to everyone, including my dad. He groaned as loud as the rest of us, just like he did every weekend. I couldn't blame him, his chores were way harder than ours. She laughed as she finally took a bite of her pancakes. "One more peep from you all and I'm going to make you clean the spit valves for the orchestra's entire brass section this afternoon." It was her favorite threat. Ewww.

"I want to go to the skateboard park," announced Luke. His legs were constantly beaten up by new scrapes. He was usually scratching at some scab and completely grossing me out.

"Fine, after you finish straightening the garage. Take your brother with you."

"Mom! I have soccer practice," Billy announced with his mouth full.

"Oh that's right. Hmm."

"Well, *I'm* going to the art museum with Malcolm," Beth said. Since she was the oldest, she liked to remind everyone how cultured she and her morose on-again-off-again boyfriend were. "There's a Chihuly glass exhibit."

"Well that sounds fun, I'll go with you," Dad piped up. I smiled. The thought of my dad and his knee socks following my sister and Malcolm around was pretty funny.

"Dad!"

"What, too cool to hang out with old Dad? Wait, I'll put on something special before we go."

"Uh-oh." I looked at Beth and giggled as she freaked out. My dad had a famous collection of hideous T-shirts. He thought the height of chic was a bright orange one that said "Some Days You're the Pigeon, Some Days You're the Statue." I usually thought they were pretty funny, unless, of course, my friends happened to be around.

Beth stared at our father in horror as one of the boys spilled juice all over the floor. Molly eagerly slurped it up, and Mom ran for the mop. The two cats were smart enough to run and hide—you'd think they'd be used to the commotion by now but apparently not. Luke righted his empty glass and then knocked over the syrup. I jumped in, hurriedly wiping up the new mess before Billy stuck his tongue in the spill. No joke, it's happened before.

"I'm going to be late. Thanks for the 'cakes." I escaped, stopping in my room on the way out the door to pick up my latest to-do list and put some of Beth's concealer on my upper lip. It looked sorta weird, but not too bad.

To Do, April 27

- Get to work on time with nothing stuck between teeth.
- Pretend Jonathan does not exist, even if he is studying three feet away, unless he tries to strike up conversation due to alluring sight of self making cappuccino.
- Buy present for Dad's b-day.
- Start homework or think of really, really good reason to ask Mrs. Peabody for an extension. (Surgery? Computer crash? Temporary amnesia? Depression over global warming?)
- Try new anti-frizz hair product. For science.

Outside, it was a perfect spring day. Wisconsin was usually freezing, but today was nice and warm. People were gardening in their small front yards and a few kids were building a skateboard ramp in someone's driveway. I glanced down at my clothes, sure I'd see a maple syrup stain somewhere. My black pants looked pretty good, but my shoes were *bor*-ing. Oh well, I like to be comfortable and none of the stuff Genna suggests that I wear ever is.

Fortunately it's a short walk to the Steeping Leaf, and within a few minutes I was there. The café is in an old stone building at the end of a bustling street filled with lots of other shops and restaurants. It has a creaky wood floor and a patio surrounded by a little stone wall topped with plants. Well-tended roses, geraniums in hanging baskets, and even a small lilac bush surrounded the cheery red door in the summer. I stopped short at the shop's front door and looked at my reflection. My hair was out of control, so I carefully put it into a low braid before crossing the threhold.

Louisa was chatting with her customers. It was a quiet morning; only three tables were full. I grinned at two young women who were visiting with my grandmother. I recognized them from the university; they were graduate students of my mom's. Denise and Meg. Fortunately, the lights were back on.

"Morning, Annie, love. You picked a good day to start."

"Good morning, Louisa." I grabbed an apron off the hook behind the counter. "Hi, Meg; hello, Denise. How are you?"

"Did your mother tell you the good news? Meg here just got a teaching position in California!" Louisa beamed at the young woman, her crystal earrings dancing happily.

"That's awesome! Congratulations, Meg!"

"Thanks, Annie. I couldn't have done it without your mom's help and recommendation. And your grandmother's tea, of course." She raised her cup to Louisa, who smiled modestly. "I think I wrote most of my dissertation here."

"Wow." The only thing I knew about dissertations was that they were *very* long. "When do you start the new job?"

"Not until the fall. I've gotta get some traveling in first," she answered.

"And I'm going with her," Denise added happily. In fact, their table was strewn with travel guides. "We're trying to map out our itinerary, and Louisa is giving us some tips from her globe-trotting days."

At this, my grandmother laughed. "It's been ages since I've gotten out of Madison for any real length of time. I doubt any of my favorite restaurants are still open halfway around the world."

"I wouldn't be so sure," Meg said, pointing to an open page in her Lonely Planet Thailand guide. "Didn't you just mention this one?" Louisa looked where she was pointing.

"Well, my goodness." Louisa fished around her apron pocket for her reading glasses. "There it is indeed." She paged through the book for a few moments, her face looking young and happy. It was like all the stress from the other day was completely gone.

"And how are your darling brothers, dear?" Louisa asked with a knowing twinkle in her eye.

Louisa is probably the only person in the world, my

mother included, who would call Billy and Luke "darling." "Mmm, messy as usual," I replied, describing how apocalyptic our family breakfast had been.

"Really?" Meg piped in disbelievingly. "Dr. Green always keeps things so perfect, that's hard to picture." I giggled, remembering the spilled juice and syrup.

"Well, even she is no match for Billy and Luke when there are sticky liquids involved," I explained. "I'm pretty sure we've never gotten through breakfast without a minor flood or trip to the emergency room." Everyone laughed.

"And how is sweet Beth?" Louisa asked.

"She's okay, I guess. She pretty much should've just gone to college *last* year, since it's all she talks about anyway," I answered. Louisa nodded in agreement.

"Well, I'm sure she'll love it when she gets there. And how about our favorite maestro? Did your mother use the whiteboard again this morning?" I nodded. It always amused Louisa to hear about her daughter running a family with a dry erase marker. In fact, the big whiteboard in the storage room was from my mom. I guess I get my list-making compulsion from her. Louisa, on the other hand, won't tell you what to do or spell it out in bullet points on a board.

Last year, when I was trying to decide if I should get braces on my teeth, Louisa was so helpful. My parents said it was up to me, (a) because they have good insurance, so it wouldn't cost them much, and (b) because my teeth weren't really that crooked. I just have this one lower tooth that's slightly wonky.

Louisa was all, "Does your wonky tooth bother you?"

"Not really. I kind of like it. But everyone is getting braces."

"Everyone?"

"Well, not Genna. But her teeth are perfect."

"Is it a good idea to get braces because everyone else is?"

"Noo . . ."

"Does getting braces hurt?"

"Yesss . . ."

"Hmm."

"Did you ever have braces, Louisa?" I asked. At this, she had laughed for a long time.

"When I was your age, Annie, the only people getting braces on their teeth were the ones with molars growing out of their foreheads. Look. I have the same wonky tooth as you." I looked. She did.

I didn't get braces.

"Let me get you some forms. I know they're around here somewhere." Louisa disappeared into her makeshift office in the corner of the storage room and came out with various wrinkled documents. She said I could fill them out later and started going over the procedures for taking orders and processing credit card payments.

"As everyone knows," Louisa said with a sigh, "it is easier to make tea out of teabags, but I like to do things the old-fashioned loose-leaf way. Keep an eye on Jonathan when you can, dear. I want to make sure he's using enough tea in each pot." My heart leapt a bit at the sound of his name. I hope Louisa didn't notice me blushing. I didn't want her to regret hiring me because I flipped out every time her other employee turned up.

Jonathan aside, I was always happy that Louisa made tea in pots, even for individual orders. Made that way, the tea leaves "bloomed" and you got a better flavor. And there's something about having your own pot of tea that just felt more special.

"Did you know that tea bags started out as samples for shop owners like your grandfather and me?" I noticed that Louisa still considered Grandpa Charles to be her partner even though he passed away four years ago. It gave me a pang because I still missed him too, very much. He always knew just the right thing to say or do, no matter what the situation. When he died, the shop lost a bit of its luster. "About a hundred years ago a merchant in

New York packaged his tea in small silk bags and saw that some of his customers were brewing it still in the bag, to avoid a mess. The rest is history; it really caught on. But true tea connoisseurs—like you and me—know that the old method is best. Now our way of doing things is the new trend . . . isn't it funny how things happen?"

Once I learned about the more technical parts of the Steeping Leaf—including how to run the incredibly scary espresso machine—the fun part began: sipping the products. I had already tried most of them, but it seemed new varieties of tea were coming out practically every day.

My mind wandered to a birthday party Louisa threw for me a few years ago. Each year, she closes the shop and throws an elaborate tea party for my friends and me; it's our special traditon. Each party is unique . . . sometimes she arranges it like a Japanese tea ceremony. Sometimes she decorates the Leaf like a Russian tearoom, complete with the exact right china. The one I am remembering now was just like afternoon tea at the Plaza. The Plaza, explained Louisa at the time, is a *very* hoity-toity hotel in New York City. Apparently they really know how to do afternoon tea. It's practically world-famous.

Louisa put her best table right in the middle of the shop, with a crisp white tablecloth and fresh flowers and everything. She had a copy of the official tea menu from the Plaza and served us finger sandwiches, clotted cream, homemade jams, and delicious petit fours. The pastries were like angel pillows and the chocolates were fit for princesses. Genna, Zoe, and I thought we had died and gone to heaven. That day, we all wore nice clothes and were extra careful with our manners, taking pains not to spill crumbs on the floor like we usually did. Louisa wore a dramatic black asymmetrical dress, just like someone in New York. She lent us all pink lipstick for the occasion as well. I didn't tell my mom that part.

"Dahling, please pass the sugar," Genna said, pretending to be a wealthy socialite who *always* had afternoon tea at the Plaza. Zoe snickered and did as she was asked. "Isn't this savory pastry to *die* for?" Gen continued. "I simply must tell my servants to learn the recipe."

Genna snapped her finger at an imaginary waiter as Louisa smiled at her. Louisa always thought my "girls" were wonderful. I couldn't help but agree. Zoe ate her sandwiches neatly as always, sighing contentedly and thanking Louisa for about the millionth time.

"Our waiter is *soo* very, very dashing. Don't you just want to *swoon*, darlings?" Genna asked, leaning back in her chair in a dramatic faint. Even at ten, she was boy crazy. She could conjure romance on a whim, probably because she was already addicted to daytime television.

"Oh yes," agreed Louisa without missing a beat. "Hans is our *most* popular waiter here at the hotel. In fact, today was supposed to be his very first day off in a whole month, but when he heard that Miss Annie was coming in for her birthday, he *insisted* on working so that he could see her. Isn't that lovely?" My grandmother winked at me as all three of us dissolved into giggles. We had four different pots of tea at the table that day, just like we would if we were really at the Plaza: jasmine blossom, lemon spice, peppermint, and English breakfast. We tried all of them, of course. Genna liked the lemon spice the best; Zoe the peppermint; and my favorite has *always* been English breakfast.

It was nice. I still remember the stacked plates of goodies and how special it felt to have the shop to myself with my best friends. Louisa had once done the same thing for my sister, Beth, on *her* birthday, but the tradition only stuck with me. Louisa said I have tea in my soul.

Anyway, this year, my party didn't happen. Genna's family was on vacation in Europe that week, and Zo got the flu at the last moment. Louisa and I still had a very nice tea together, but I hoped that the tradition wouldn't fade away. As soon as I learned the finer points of how Louisa ran her store, I promised myself that this year I'd arrange a very special tea for my grandmother. After all, I was getting old enough to do it for *her*. The thought warmed me up. I'd read up a bit on famous tea services and surprise her as soon as I could. I wondered where one could find truffle mayonnaise.

I was snapped out of my daydreaming by someone on the patio making faces in our front window. As I got closer, I saw that it was Zach Anderson. His annoying popped collar and preppy faux-hawk made me grimace, even from a distance. He put his open mouth on the glass and blew his face up, getting slobber everywhere. What was *he* doing here? On my first day! Louisa didn't notice him because she had returned to Meg's table for more guidebook flipping. I decided I would handle my first workplace crisis by myself. I grabbed a white towel from our sink and went outside.

"What is *wrong* with you?" I said to Zach, swatting at him with the towel.

"Green! Is that an *apron*? Are you *working*?"

"If you must know, yes, I am." Even with Zach Anderson in my presence, it was hard not to smile. I was just so happy to be there. And proud of my apron, if you want to know the truth.

"Aw. It's so sad when people have to use child labor to keep their businesses open. Don't you get an allowance?"

"Not everyone was born into the Trump family, stupid,"

I answered, wishing I had more time to give him a proper lecture on wasteful extravagance and the starving children in the third world.

"Well, I suppose if you did have an allowance, you'd just spend it on something dumb, like *tea*." He mimicked sipping out of a teacup with his pinky out.

"Tea isn't dumb, you diseased amoeba. If you aren't going to buy anything, go stink up someone else's patio." I was getting good and warmed up now.

"Touchy, touchy!" he taunted.

"Don't you have anywhere else to be? Why are you always around?" Why *was* he always around? "Go slobber on some *other* window!"

"Fine. I'm telling everyone this place has E. coli. See ya!" He hopped on his thousand-dollar bike and sped off, leaving me steaming. I wiped up his disgusting spit and went to the sink to wash my hands. Three times.

A couple of moments later a customer who looked as if she had just stepped out of a salon came in and asked for a noncaffeinated tea, something fruity. I suggested one of the popular herbal varieties, called Mango Blossom.

"That sounds perfect, I'll take a cup to go," she replied. I was so proud, I hadn't even needed Louisa's help to complete the order and ring it all up.

Luckily, I know my tea. I understood that black and

green had caffeine while herbal did not. Actually, herbal tea wasn't really tea because it didn't come from the tea plant. Did you know that? It's true. I knew chamomile was good for soothing stress, and ginseng was good for strengthening the immune system. I planned to become, like my grandmother, extremely healthy and filled with positive energy thanks to spending time here (well, positive as long as Zach didn't show up again). It was exciting. For me, tea was more than tea. It was tradition. It was family. Soul medicine, Louisa and I liked to say. She returned to the area behind the counter.

"We do a tea of the day now, which is discounted. That was Jonathan's idea." Louisa pointed to a black-board near the register. Today it was Peach Paradise. He was smart *and* cute.

"So, um, where is Jonathan?" I asked, not looking directly at Louisa. "He seems very nice."

"Oh, he doesn't work today." Even though I could tell that Louisa probably suspected my crush, she decided not to say anything. She was wonderful like that. "Anyway, the key thing is remembering the customers' preferences. Now, I've been doing this for a very long time and I still forget on occasion. And believe me, they take it personally. I'll show you my cheat sheet." Louisa grinned conspiratorially and pointed to a little index card under the register. It had amusing descriptions of the regulars, along with their drink of choice. Some had names; some did not. "Mustache man: Decaf green." "Yoga lady: Raspberry blend." "Tan nose (Greg): Double espresso."

Practically everyone in the whole neighborhood knew Louisa and remembered my grandfather. Grandpa Charles had been a professor in the botany department at the university, where he specialized mainly in ancient herbs and their medicinal properties. He and Louisa opened the shop almost exactly thirty years ago, after his sabbatical in Japan. Louisa had fallen in love with the Japanese teahouses and wanted to bring a small part of that culture home with her to Madison. When my mom was a teenager, *she* worked here. The teashop has always been primarily Louisa's baby, but my grandfather was the driving force in getting prominent Madisonians to come in and bring their friends. I know my mom worried a lot about how having him gone was affecting the shop. Louisa was extremely warm and friendly but she wasn't quite as gregarious as her late husband had been. She could often be found meditating quietly instead of out on the town.

"'Tan nose'?" I giggled.

"You'll see. Ooh, look, your second customer. Go to it!" Louisa stepped back and pretended to rearrange some cups. I smiled at the young mother standing before me with her toddler.

"Hello. What can I get for you today?"

"Hi there. I'll take a large iced tea to go and one order of cucumber sandwiches," she said to me. Then, "How are you, Louisa?"

"I'm doing very well, thank you, Ling. I'd like to introduce you to our newest barista, my granddaughter Annie." I smiled and we shook hands. "And how is little Hieu?" The toddler was looking around but probably wouldn't be quiet for very long. I remembered where the iced tea was brewed and easily filled up a large cup. Louisa prepared the sandwiches without even looking as she chatted. I waved at Hieu, who stared at me uncertainly.

"Oh, good. But with him walking now, I feel as if I'm constantly trying to keep a mini tornado in one place," Ling replied, sounding tired.

"I remember those days. You always have to watch out for those angelic-looking ones." Louisa handed Ling her sandwiches and bent down to talk to Hieu.

"Now, you be a good boy for your mama, young man," she said, cooing to him as he stared back innocently, blinking his big eyes. I noticed she placed a small cookie into his eager hand at no charge. Ling gathered her sandwiches and her son and headed back out, looking refreshed as she sipped her tea.

It wasn't hard at all to be a barista. I was already loving the fact that I could make someone's day better with a cookie or cup of tea . . . no wonder the Leaf's chi was so positive! My grandmother continued with her instructions. "There are a few special customers, as you know. There's an elderly couple who comes in almost every day dressed in matching outfits. They order one pot of Earl Grey and strike up conversations with young people."

"Oh, Mr. and Mrs. Kopinski, sure. Last time I was here, I talked to them about the bike trail. They got matching bicycles at Willy Street."

"Lovely," Louisa replied. "Oops, here's some more customers for you." I poured coffee for two retirees and wiped up the counter, which was already spotlessly clean. It had only been two hours, but I already loved my job.

Another customer stepped up to the counter. "Medium extra-whip, soy chai latte." *Whoa.* I looked at Louisa in a panic.

"Isn't this weather lovely?" Louisa could steam milk and talk meteorology at once. I tried to absorb what she was doing with the scary machine behind the counter.

"It sure is," the customer replied. "I'll take a hundred more days like these."

"Okay, here's your drink, Ray." He took it with a wave and headed back outside.

"Don't worry, you'll get the hang of it, my sweet."

We chatted amiably and as things quieted down, Louisa asked me about Gen and Zoe. I promised they would come in for a visit soon.

Our elderly book reader came in, this time holding a copy of something called *A Moveable Feast*. I decided to officially introduce myself. It wouldn't do for the Steeping Leaf's regular customers to think of me just as "the owner's granddaughter," now that I was a proper barista and all.

"Hello, sir. I'm Annie, Louisa's granddaughter and the newest barista." I presented my hand and he took it. His grip was firm yet gentle.

"Charles Shanahan's granddaughter! Why I'll be . . . I'm Frank Silverman. How do you do?"

"I'm great, Mr. Silverman. Nice to meet you." I smiled at him.

"You know, I was once good friends with your grandfather. We traded books for, oh, I'd say twenty years."

"Really? He gave me books, too, when I was little. What are you reading today?" It pleased me to think that my grandfather's library of books had homes on shelves scattered throughout Madison.

"Oh, one of my favorites," he said as he showed me the spine. "Hemingway. It's about Paris. My second-favorite city."

"Your second favorite? What's your first?" Louisa brought over Mr. Silverman's usual, a steaming cup of oolong, and smiled at both of us. I could see she was pleased I was chatting with Grandpa's old friend.

"Why, this one of course. What's your favorite?" he asked.

"Madison too. But I haven't been that many places yet." Just Florida to see my other grandparents and Chicago a few times.

"Oh trust me, you will. But you'll always love your home." He sipped his tea and smiled at me. I knew that he probably wanted to start reading his book, but I couldn't resist one more question. I'm like that sometimes.

"So how many times have you been to Paris?"

"Too many to count! I have an apartment there. In the Latin quarter. In fact, there's a shop there that is much like your grandmother's here. *Si parva lecit componere magnis.*"

"Wow! That is amazing." I looked at Mr. Silverman quizzically and he translated his Latin for me. The phrase, from the poet Virgil, meant "if one may compare small things with great." It made me so happy to think there was another place like the Leaf all the way across the globe, in a spot as glamorous as Paris. Wait till I told Genna! She'd want to do a Teashop Girls field trip. My mom would love that. Not.

I cleared a table of a pot and two empty cups. Out of the corner of my eye, I noticed someone behaving impatiently at the counter, tapping his foot and looking for something . . . or someone. He had an official look about him—kind of like an annoyed school vice principal. He held a document in his hand and wore a scowl on his face.

I rushed over to the register to take his order. "Good afternoon, sir. What can I get you today?"

"Louisa Shanahan?"

"That's my grandmother. I think she's out back. Can I help you?"

"I need to speak to the shop's owner."

I was trying my best to be super helpful, but nothing could placate him. Just then Louisa appeared behind me.

"I'm the owner."

"You're Louisa Shanahan?"

"Yes?"

"This is an eviction notice. You have thirty days to pay your back rent or you must vacate the premises."

Tea balls are a way of packaging tea into small, spherical bags. You can still buy packaged tea balls today, or you can put your loose tea into a little round mesh metal tea ball. They make ones that are big enough for a whole pot or small enough for just a cup.

When you're having a hard day, remember...

there's

QUICK COMFORT

in a cup of TENDER LEAF TEA!

With **housework** harder work than ever these days, you're not forgetting, are you?, that there's *quick comfort* in a cup of Tender Leaf Tea. It warms you u,, it cheers you up, and it tastes simply wonderful.

Make your cup of quick comfort with a Tender Leaf Tea Ball... and there's no pot to bother with, no strainer, no long wait. Never a speck in the cup, and no stray leaves. Tender Leaf Brand Tea Balls *filler!*

Next time, try America's largest-selling tea balls...

TENDER LEAF TEA BALLS

TENDER LEAF
Brand
Tea Balls
Orange Pekoe and Pekoe

Chapter Six

Remember the tea kettle—
it is always up to its neck in hot water, yet it still sings.
—AUTHOR UNKNOWN

I rushed back to the storeroom once the last of the customers had gone. There were no windows in the back, so I had to be careful not to run into anything. Crates of inventory were still scattered all around from yesterday. It seemed things were worse than just one unpaid electricity bill. I wonder if my mom knew. I felt scared, not sure what to do at all. I cleared my throat when I entered Louisa's office.

"Um, Louisa? Is everything okay?" I asked very softly. I didn't know exactly how things worked when you rented a building, but it seemed there had to be a mix-up. They had to come over and get this straightened out right away. "Did you call the property owner? This has got to be some terrible mistake. Louisa? Louisa?" My grandmother was making no move to call anyone, even though I was holding out the phone feebly.

"Oh, Annie. I miss your grandfather." Louisa said this very quietly. I took a seat by awkwardly placing some manila folders on the floor and squeezing onto a chair. Even though some meditation music played quietly, neither one of us was very soothed. It was so strange to see an adult so sad. I had always figured middle school was the worst, and it pretty much got steadily better from there. Maybe not.

"I miss him too." I paused. It felt good to remember him out loud like I had with Mr. Silverman; Louisa and I hadn't talked about him in a long time. From the look on Louisa's face, I wasn't sure what was going on, but it was clear there would be no calling the landlord. At least not right away.

"You know, even after he died, I could feel his presence here with me. We shared so many good times in the shop that I was always able to believe he was just around the corner, checking in back for a new shipment of rooibos or out on the patio chatting with a favorite customer." I knew Louisa was in her shop practically from the time she got up until the time she went to bed. "But now . . .

I'm starting to lose that feeling. And, as it turns out, the shop as well." Louisa sighed.

"What do you mean?"

"I shouldn't be burdening you with this on your first day. I thought things would have turned around by now."

"Louisa, you can tell me anything, really."

"The truth is, the Steeping Leaf is in big trouble. We can't pay our bills or our rent. I had no business hiring you, dearheart."

"Don't say that!"

"It's been wonderful to have you here—even for just a day." Louisa smiled and seemed to gather herself. "Annie, I know I've explained to you many times how to live like a river, clear and undisturbed as things unfold. The shop's struggle is a rapids we must flow around. We cannot know what the future will bring." She was oddly serene.

"I don't understand . . ." The river stuff made sense to me when we were talking about dealing with mean people at school, but I wasn't feeling very peaceful about the idea of the shop closing. I didn't see how my grandmother could be so calm about it.

"There will always be tea, dear. Perhaps there will not always be the Steeping Leaf. But there will always be tea. And maybe this is just a sign that it's time for me to do like other people my age and move to a warm spot. Approach a new phase in life." I looked at her in horror. Louisa leave Madison . . . there were no words. As my mind raced anxiously, she rustled for something in her desk. "I found something for your handbook." She handed me a rare tea card, an advertisement that looked to be many decades old. I took it happily but couldn't shake my frown over my grandmother's Zen calmness.

"Listen, Louisa. It wasn't a mistake to hire me. I promise it wasn't. I'll work for free if I have to." Louisa gave me a small smile. "We are going to bring this place back. So, maybe some people have forgotten about us . . . we'll remind them. I'm sure my parents could help."

"No, no, Annie. I cannot trouble your mother and father. I won't."

"But—"

"Really, I'd prefer you not mention it, dear. They certainly have enough on their plates." I knew what my grandmother was saying was true—my parents *did* have a lot on their plates—but they also loved Louisa like I did and would be upset to know what was going on. I felt terribly torn and confused. What could I do instead of telling my mom? I thought for a moment. "What about all the customers who love you? Mr. Silverman and Meg and the Kopinskis? Surely they will want to help."

"They do help, Annie. Just by coming in. But I'm afraid we just don't have quite as many regulars as we used to. And I would never dream of discussing money matters with the ones who remain." She was firm. It was hard for me to accept. Hardly a month went by that Louisa wasn't buying piles of Girl Scout cookies from someone's niece in the neighborhood or giving someone a little short of change a free scone. It seemed to me it was the neighborhood's turn to help *her*.

"You can't move away," I said a bit desperately. "So many people love you. Mom and Dad and Luke and Billy and Beth love you," and for added emphasis, "Ling and Hieu, and Meg, and Denise, and Greg with the tan nose love you. And the Teashop Girls. The Teashop Girls love you, too! Remember the Teashop Girls, Louisa?"

"How are sweet Genna and Zoe? It seems like it's been ages since I've seen them."

I swallowed hard. My friends were just like everyone else. They had forgotten about the Leaf. But now, in its time of need, they would have to remember. And come back. They'd just have to. It was up to us. Genna was just going to have to stop thinking about boys for a minute and help drag customers in. Wait! Maybe she could just start dragging boys in. They followed her everywhere else.

"They're still around, Louisa. Just a little busy. But don't worry. The Teashop Girls are going to save the Leaf. I promise."

Genna, in fact, had not been kidding when she announced she would come up wth a plan. She called me excitedly the moment I got home, just as we decided the day before.

"Okay, I got the chalk and I've got Zoe. Meet us at the corner of Monroe and Commonwealth in ten."

"Cool." Genna's plan was actually pretty good. I was *sure* it would improve the situation at the Leaf. It wasn't very Zen of us, but this was one instance where letting the ying and yang of the universe push us around like river pebbles was just not the answer. As I approached our corner, I could already see Zoe dressed in all white. She had come directly from a tennis match. I had a feeling her clothes weren't going to stay sparkling clean if Genna had anything to do with it.

"Hey, ladies. Check this out." I showed them the new tea advertisement Louisa had given me.

"Wow," Zoe said. "How many of those do you have now?"

"Correction: *We* have over a hundred." I smiled at her. "How was your match?"

"Pretty good. I'm trying to get the whole team to

switch from Gatorade to iced tea." She grinned. "I figure every little bit helps."

"Oh, definitely," I agreed. Genna was hopping around behind me, eager to get started on her plan. She had decided that we should combine advertising with art and make some chalkings in the neighborhood. Zoe and I couldn't draw very well, but we were going to follow Genna around writing slogans like "Had Your Tea Today?" near her illustrations of teapots and things. It would be fun.

Monroe Street looked so pretty as twilight approached. Several families were out and about enjoying the weekend, making their way to Michael's Frozen Custard for turtle sundaes or down to the park on Lake Wingra to put their feet in the water and to spend some time on the swing sets. We saw a young college-age couple holding hands and a group of people on bicycles. Gen waved to someone she knew from her theater.

Most of the streets in our neighborhood were named after ex-presidents. There's Grant, and Harrison, and Jefferson, and Garfield. Monroe Street is one of Madison's most special spots, like State Street in between the university and our city's capitol square. State Street has no cars on it. The mile-long stretch has changed a lot lately (which my mom groans about constantly), with local shops and restaurants switching to chain stores. I was worried that it wouldn't look so interesting in ten more years. I was also worried that my very own neighborhood was experiencing the same kinds of changes. What would happen to hometown proprietors like my grandmother? I was relieved we were doing *something*, even if it was small.

"Okay, Zo, you can have the white chalk," Gen said diplomatically, knowing how much our friend loved staying spotless. "Annie, you can pick whatever you want. I thought we'd pretty much stick to the sidewalks around here."

"Great!" I exclaimed. Genna was already busy drawing something, so Zoe and I smiled and started chalking out messages around her. It was almost as fun as our old weekly afternoon teatime. Genna's drawings were amazing. I knew people would stop and notice them.

"So, Gen, what shows are they putting on this summer in Spring Green?" Zoe asked. "Annie and I will definitely go if you're in one. If my stepdad says it's okay." Last year, we saw *A Midsummer Night's Dream*. Genna played Mustardseed, one of Queen Titania's fairies. Since the American Players Theatre is an outdoor theater, the production was incredible . . . real stars and a full moon made it so magical.

"Ooh, yay! Um, *Much Ado About Nothing* and *The Merchant of Venice*. I adore *Ado*! 'Against my will, I am sent to bid you come into dinner.'" Zoe and I smiled at each other as Genna began quoting the play, bowing deeply and doing two different voices for the characters. "'*Fair Beatrice, thank you for your pains.*' 'I took no more pains for those thanks than you take pains to thank me. If it had been painful, I would not have come.' '*You take pleasure then in the message?*' 'Yea, just so much as you may take upon a knife's point. You have no stomach, signor? Fare you well.' '*Ha. "Against my will I am sent to bid you come into dinner." There's a double meaning in that.*'"

"Bravo! Bravo!" I said, clapping loudly in the street as Zoe giggled. Genna took a deep bow.

We covered four blocks in an hour; then I had to get home. I gave Gen what was left of the chalk and brushed off my pants, which were no longer completely black.

Walking back home, I read over our handiwork.

Had Your Tea Today? The sidewalk asked me over and over again. *Why yes,* I answered back happily. *Yes, I have.*

" Japan Green Tea is A World Treasure "

This is the tea trade card Louisa gave me most recently. Isn't it beautiful? Tea manufacturers and tea-shop owners made cards featuring their tea, and people like me have been collecting them for generations. We're called "cartophilists." Sometimes the cards have pretty artwork, like this one, or sometimes they have the name and address of a shop. They were always meant to be part of a set, to encourage people to buy more and get a complete collection. I think the Steeping Leaf should make trade cards, maybe with Genna's drawings. Don't you agree?

Chapter Seven

Sipping thoughts of peace, hope floats my way.
—MOONLIGHT SPICE TEA BAG

Exactly two hours after we finished our lovely tea chalkings, it started to rain. And not just rain, it was a torrential downpour of hurricanic proportions. All three of us had conveniently forgotten to check the weather. After wailing to each other on IM, we were very discouraged. None of our ideas were going to work, because we didn't have, like, an advertising budget or driver's licenses. We needed new ideas, and fast, but not one of us came up with anything good.

Louisa refused to talk to me anymore about the eviction notice. She insisted that everything was fine and that I could work whenever I wanted to. I didn't really believe her and was terrified that she was secretly looking at retirement villas or monasteries in Asia that catered to old people. (*Were* there monasteries in Asia for old people? I hoped not.) I encouraged the customers we still had to "come back soon!" without even thinking.

When I tried to ask about money, she would just change the subject.

"Louisa, how much more per month do you think we need to make?"

"Oh Annie, sweetie. Such talk! Did you see our robin hatched her chicks? Look." I looked. She had. But I honestly was having a hard time getting as tickled about that as my grandmother seemed to be. "Also, Mr. Silverman brought me a book to give you. Let me see . . ."

She rustled through the shelves under the counter for a minute and produced a gorgeous leather bound Jane Austen title, *Mansfield Park*. I tucked it into my canvas tote and opened my mouth to ask again about the Leaf's rent, but by then Louisa was greeting Ling and Hieu, who arrived with a racket, and I knew it was hopeless. Hieu was throwing a fit, crying like the world was about to end. I kinda knew how he felt. Ling tried to shush him with a plastic toy in the stroller, but it wasn't working.

"Is he still teething, dear?" Louisa asked over the din.

"I think so," Ling replied. "Or we have a *Rosemary's Baby* situation on our hands. What've you got?" Hieu continued to fuss, though slightly more quietly after Louisa handed Hieu a large, dense cookie to gnaw on.

"Annie, can you fetch my book?" Louisa asked, as she gathered up some different herbs behind us. I didn't know what Ling meant by "Rosemary's baby," but I did as my grandmother asked, quickly. She had a favorite herbal remedy book and probably wanted to double check it even though I knew she had most of it memorized. She flipped to the right page and prepared two packages for Ling. I tried smiling at Hieu and waving his toy, but it didn't help much. I still had a lot to learn. Louisa handed over the herbal concoctions. "One of these is for the baby," Louisa explained to Ling. "You won't need to give him much at all." She explained how to prepare a sweet herb paste to rub on his sore gums. "The other is for you, dear. It's a tea. To help you sleep, should you ever get the chance."

Ling looked very grateful. As much as my grandmother's refusal to talk money frustrated me, I was awed by her. I could see she almost forgot to charge Ling for the herbs. (She did, though.) Mother and son headed for the door, both looking much calmer than they had when they came in.

I talked to my parents about the situation at the shop, sheepishly, because I knew Louisa didn't want me to. They said they would think about how they could help, but I knew they were already worried about paying for Beth's college in the fall. Instead of going to UW (Go Badgers!), where my mom could get her free tuition, Beth had to go choose a small, pricey East Coast liberal arts college. *Note to self:* If you want to have piles of money lying around when you get old, don't have four kids. Meanwhile, my mind raced with possible plans to increase business and save the store. How could we get that rent money? And fast?

To Do, May 10

- Figure out a way to get the Steeping Leaf on the Travel Channel. Or something.
- Convince Beth to go to school here and give Louisa her tuition $. Yeah, right.
- Ask Mrs. Peabody to check Zach's locker again, as smelliness in that general area has not decreased.
- Buy Dad's birthday present. Soon. Gah!

Almost two weeks had gone by since my first day, and so far, the power had stayed on. Even in the middle of the day at school, practically all I thought about was the Leaf and its bills. In algebra, x was the Leaf's profit. Louisa had scraped together enough to pay a portion of the back rent. I could tell she was still very worried though. Things were precarious. The phone rang a lot and suppliers were on the other end, demanding back payments. I felt so helpless. Jonathan was the one bright spot in all of this, and even that wasn't going so well. I came in a little early for my shifts to see him, "volunteering" for a half hour since we were rarely on the schedule together. He didn't seem to be falling in love with me like he was supposed to. Rather, a typical conversation between us was more like this:

Me: So, my cousin in Los Angeles works as this assistant to a movie producer. Isn't that cool?

Jonathan: Uh-huh.

Me: She says that famous rich people don't like eating their vegetables, even though they pretty much have to in order to stay skinny. So they put them in smoothies and order them all wrapped up in these fancy little sushi roles soaked in wasabi. It seems like an awful lot of work to get an asparagus spear to go down, if you ask me. Do you like sushi?

Jonathan: Sure.

Me: Me too, but only if it's cooked.

Jonathan: Then it's not really sushi.

Me: Oh. Yeah. I guess not.

Still, I was totally crushing. I stared at him as he finished up his shift duties and tried to figure out what he was thinking. I decided to bring up the Steeping Leaf's problems with him. That was something we had in common. Since Genna and Zoe and I didn't have anything else up our sleeves at the moment, maybe Jonathan and I could somehow save the shop together. It would be so romantic. Anyway, it was better than hanging around worrying and doing nothing.

"Um, Jonathan? I've noticed the shop isn't as busy as it used to be. I'm worried."

"Tell me about it. We seriously need to cut costs or this place is history."

"What if we just sold more tea?"

"That would be good too. But we can't afford to advertise. And we also can't afford to buy half the supplies we need. We're almost out of espresso beans. I can't believe

I decided to make this place my econ project. I am so screwed."

"Your what?"

"Econ project. I have to write a major paper for one of my classes about a local business, but this is more like a local joke."

"But . . . but . . ." Okay, this is embarrassing, but my eyes filled with tears. How could he *say* such a thing?

"Look, Annie. I don't mean to sound like I don't care. I just think it is going to take more than good chi to put this place back on track. I'm sorry, but Zen monks don't have to deal with a corporate coffee conglomerate. We do." I sighed and looked sadly across the street at the coffeehouse with its steady stream of customers going in and out.

"I want to do something too! Let's tell everyone their coffee gives you back hair."

"Ha, right. What we really need to do is go in there, take notes, and copy everything they do down to the overpriced mocha brownies. It's a business model that really works." Jonathan had a look of admiration on his face; I felt confused. Copy them? What was he *talking* about? I glanced around the teashop at the well-worn furniture, packed shelves, and walls full of travel posters curling at the edges. The Steeping Leaf was a million times better than any stupid big coffee chain. I opened my mouth to protest but stopped myself. He was so, so . . . so completely adorable when he got excited. "Huh," was all I managed to blurt out.

"No, seriously."

"Seriously what?"

"Let's go tonight after this place closes. They are open way later, you know. Take a few notes. Spy. We, the younger generation, need to show your grandmother how things work these days. Longer hours, less product, higher prices. She needs to see that the Steeping Leaf has to join the twenty-first century."

"Um."

"I'll meet you there at eight, after you've closed up." He tossed his rag on the counter and grabbed his backpack. I couldn't believe that I was being asked on what could potentially be a *date* . . . to the boring, sterile, overpriced coffee factory across the street.

But hey, it was better than nothing. I smiled bigger than I had since Louisa hired me.

Louisa's Very Best Spiced Blueberry Scones

INGREDIENTS

2 cups organic whole wheat flour
1 tablespoon baking powder
⅓ cup sugar
½ teaspoon salt
½ teaspoon cinnamon
½ teaspoon ground ginger

6 tablespoons unsalted butter
1 teaspoon vanilla extract
1 egg
½ cup half-and-half
¾ cup fresh blueberries, rinsed
½ cup clotted cream

Preheat the oven to 375 degrees F. Grease baking sheet.
Combine all the dry ingredients (flour, baking powder, sugar, salt, cinnamon, and ginger) in a large bowl and mix well.
In a different bowl, combine the butter (room temperature), vanilla, egg, and half-and-half and mix well. Stir into dry ingredients.
Gently fold in the blueberries.
Place the dough on a floured surface and roll out to 1 inch thick.
   Cut into 2-inch triangles and put them on greased baking sheet.
Bake for 20 minutes or until golden brown.
Serve warm with clotted cream.
Makes 18 scones.

Chapter Eight

Coffee is not my cup of tea.

—SAMUEL GOLDWYN

I had an upcoming world history essay due for social studies, so I decided to write everything I could find out about tea that weekend. You could say I was obsessed, but I prefer "focused." I was IMing with Genna at the same time, which I'm sure my teacher would love if she knew. Hey, I'm learning to multitask young. It was after midnight, directly after my big date—more on that in a second, I know you're curious. I got all my major points written down and decided to fill the rest in tomorrow once I read a few more sources. We were supposed to organize our writing chronologically this time, so I tried to keep all my tea facts in order by when they happened. I knew I would add my essay to the Handbook as soon as it was graded.

Excerpt from . . .

THE HISTORY OF TEA
by Annie Green

Emperor Shen-Nung discovered tea in China by accident in 2737 B.C. It was the national drink of China for thousands of years before being introduced to Japan in A.D. 800 by Buddhist monks. People used it as a medicine for the next five hundred years. The Japanese tea ceremony was developed and was considered an art form. They used only the green variety and had special tearooms where people entered on their knees. Japanese people used tea to help with meditation and reflection, parts of their religion. They believed that each meeting of friends for tea was very special because the particular circumstances of the day would never be repeated.

In the sixteenth century, tea traders spread tea throughout Asia, Russia, and Europe. Sailors who drank tea during their journeys were healthier than those who didn't. Queen Elizabeth I drank tea in the morning. Catherine of Portugal married Charles II in 1662 and spread the tea craze. Her dowry included the island of Bombay. Charles leased it to the East India Company. It had a monopoly on tea trade for many years. Royalty and upper classes developed a high tea tradition of serving at four p.m. Tea became the national drink of England.

I decided to add some stuff about tea history in the United States, too. Did you know that tea was first brought to the American colonies by the Dutch? Back in the 1600s, when New York was called New Amsterdam, the tiny colony there drank more tea than *all* of England. Early Americans really loved tea. The Boston Tea Party happened because they were super mad over a tea tax. I found it *very* inspiring. If the patriots could fight for American independence to keep tea affordable (okay, a tiny stretch of the truth), we could certainly save the Steeping Leaf. It would be un-American not to!

I stopped doing homework for the millionth time and thought about my weird experience with Jonathan. A teeny part of me—the annoying part that always spoke the truth—was willing to admit that had *not* been a date. At all.

"Okay, so what I'm saying is that we need to scale back on the tea stuff and focus more on espresso beverages.

People are caffeine junkies; tea isn't wired enough. You know? Write that down, okay?"

Jonathan led me through the two-story store that had opened mere months before. It smelled so new. Everything was shiny. Too shiny. We were standing at the counter, sipping really, really strong coffee. I tried not to make a face as I took tiny tastes. I kept wondering when we'd sit down and start talking like normal people. The Leaf was *so* much better. We had feng shui! I didn't see any flow here at all. The line was too long. I seriously doubted that the stressed out store manager placed potted plants around with as much care as my grandmother and I had done. Come to think of it, there *were* no potted plants.

"Also, I think Louisa should consider getting more uniform tables and chairs."

"But our furniture is so comfortable," I sputtered. I remembered how the regular customers had their favorite spots, gravitating not only to the same couch again and again but to the same spot *on* the couch. Some of the cushion stains even had really funny stories to tell, like the time Zach Anderson showed up and challenged me to a chess match. I beat the pants off of him in, like, four minutes and he was so indignant, he spilled his drink all over the place. I still smile every time I see that particular blob. So does Louisa.

"Yeah, I know. People sit in it for hours after ordering only one thing. Less comfortable would be good."

"Oh."

"Listen, Annie. Your grandmother is going to need some convincing, but this is our only chance at saving the Leaf. I think she'll really listen to you if you echo my advice on this stuff. I'd hate to see her go out of business forever." Jonathan was very solemn, even with his long hair flopping in his face.

"I would too. That place is like home to me." In a quieter voice I said, "And my friends." I tried not to think about the fact that neither Genna nor Zoe had come in since I started work. It seemed like that day we were chalking, things might return to the good old days of the Teashop Girls. Then the stupid rain had to ruin it, and Gen had to get all busy running out to Spring Green for theater stuff, and Zoe had to practice her serve ten hours per day.

As if things could get any worse on my "date," I spotted my favorite person sitting in the corner. Zach. Ugh. It was completely unsurprising that Zach would hang out here. So unoriginal. He was with one of his friends, turning straw wrappers into spitballs. Lovely. I tried to avoid making eye contact, but he spotted me. Why couldn't he find one of the zillion franchises that wasn't in *my* neighborhood? Of course he had to get right up and come over and bother me. I couldn't *believe* I would have to admit knowing someone so childish in front of Jonathan.

"Annie Green, teashop traitor! I see you've come in for superior products and service." I gave him my very best withering stare. Fortunately, Jonathan had wandered away for a minute and was intently looking at the unremarkable CDs by the sugar and cream bar.

"Hi, Zach. Shouldn't you be doing homework? I hear you're getting a D in math."

"Ha. I thought I'd come check out my future neighborhood." He looked around, pleased with himself. *What?*

"Excuse me?" Zach Anderson in my neighborhood? OMG. Wasn't the universe cruel enough, making me see him every day at school?

"Yeah. My parents are developing a new building here." He was very smug. Zach liked to hint a lot about how rich he was. His parents were real-estate tycoons, which I guess made him the Condo Prince. *Gag.* "We might move in, which, of course, would be a huge downgrade from Shorewood but would completely up the value of the development."

I decided to ignore his snide "downgrade" comment and just remind myself that some people had no social skills whatsoever. "Might? Does that mean might *not*?" I asked, hopefully.

"So welcoming. *Tsk-tsk.* Who is *that*?" Zach noticed Jonathan; it was clearly time to end this conversation and get out of there.

"No one. See you later." I walked away from my horrid classmate and returned to Jonathan, hoping to steer us toward the door.

"I think you're right about . . . stuff. Perhaps we should give the Leaf an update." I bit my lip a little as I said it.

"Good. I think we can really streamline things, and it'll all be fine. Take a peek in the bathroom." He gestured toward the door. I looked at him doubtfully, still inching out. I had seen plenty of gross public restrooms in my life. Was this really necessary? He opened the door to the women's room himself and pointed.

"See? No French soaps. No thick towels that have to be hand-washed. No flowers, and certainly no free hard candy. This is what I'm talking about. From now on, Dial and paper."

"I like the French soap. It smells like lilacs."

"And costs seven bucks a pound. I checked. I'm glad we came here, Annie. It's good for everyone who is part of the Steeping Leaf to see the direction the business needs to take to survive. The only constant is change, you know. Someone wise said that. Probably Bill Gates."

"Um, wow." My voice was flat. Jonathan was looking *much* less cute.

This clipping is from 1898. The story of tea in Ceylon, which is now the nation of Sri Lanka, is really interesting. The island used to grow only coffee, but then a fungus destroyed the crop and the landowners panicked. Fortunately, a man from Scotland named James Taylor realized the climate was right for growing tea. So he did, and it was a huge success. Pretty soon the island of Ceylon was producing tens of thousands of tons of tea. That's a lot of tea! I wonder if I should put a copy of this clipping in my History of Tea essay . . .

Chapter Nine

Bread and water can so easily be toast and tea.

—AUTHOR UNKNOWN

The next day, after we both arrived at the shop after school, Jonathan presented all his opinions and ideas to Louisa. She sat quietly and nodded her head in that meditative way of hers while I brewed a pot of rosehip tea for a couple of college students with dreadlocks. I could overhear Jonathan making his case for improvements. I expected my grandmother to wave him off, but instead I heard Louisa call my name.

"Annie? Darling, can you come over here a minute?" I wiped my hands, smiled at my customers, and went over to Louisa and Jonathan. "The young man here wants to save my store."

"I know, Louisa. We both do." I remembered my promise about the Teashop Girls and felt ashamed it had been over two weeks since we did the sidewalk chalkings and we hadn't come up with anything good since. At least Jonathan was doing something to save the shop. We had basically let a little weather and full schedules stop us. Not exactly on the level of the American Revolutionaries.

"What do you think about all this?" Louisa gestured to Jonathan's laptop. A PowerPoint presentation was on the monitor. Jonathan made eye contact with me and smiled. I wondered if he had any idea how my stomach acted when he did that.

"It looks very professional."

"Professional, yes. I suppose you're right about that. In any case, what do you think about changing this place a bit? Giving the Leaf a bit of a facelift?" She looked carefully at my face, ready to read my true feelings regardless of what I said.

"Sure, Louisa. It sounds good." I knew that Jonathan wanted more than a facelift. But I kept my mouth shut and put a bright smile on my face. Something had to be done, after all. Probably something even more dramatic than sweeping up the dust bunnies, which I did earlier. "I'm happy to help however I can."

"That's my sweet, sweet girl. Isn't she a sweet girl, Jonathan?" I felt my face blush a deep shade of crimson. Though I very desperately wanted Jonathan to agree with my grandmother, I felt strange. The last thing I wanted was for the Steeping Leaf to look like the competition. And now that's just what I said I would help do. For a moment, I looked down at my feet. Then I felt a hand on my shoulder. It was Jonathan's. A warm feeling flooded through me.

"Yeah. She's terrific."

I understood, at that moment, why Genna loved boys so much. I gulped.

All About Japanese Tea Ceremonies

The Tea Ceremony isn't just a break in the day for a beverage or a meal. It's actually more of an art. There's this museum in Seattle that has a whole tearoom right inside, so people can see for themselves how beautiful a tea ceremony can be. I heard you can't actually go inside it, though. I guess you might have to visit Japan for that.

The ceremony itself evolved from a Zen Buddhist custom. It's a series of rituals performed in a certain, perfect order. The idea is to honor your friends and the harmony of the universe using the four principles of harmony, respect, purity, and tranquility.

Masters of the tea ceremony must train for many, many years. People taking part in the ceremony must wash their hands and feet and stoop low when entering the room, to show their humility. Those at the ceremony don't talk very much like Zoe, Genna, and I do, because they are too busy enjoying the smells of the matcha green tea preparation and the graceful movements of the master. I hope someday I'll get to go to a real tea ceremony . . .

Chapter Ten

If man has no tea in him, he is incapable
of understanding truth and beauty.

—JAPANESE PROVERB

That weekend, I am pretty sure I worked harder than I ever had in my entire life, except for maybe that time my mom insisted we have a garage sale. Along with Jonathan and Louisa and my sister, Beth, I cleared every surface in the Steeping Leaf. We took all the posters down and scraped years of paint off the walls. We removed all the mismatched jars and books from the shelves and replaced them with two-dozen standard, sealed clear bins. The oldest furniture got moved to storage and we painted the walls a sort of bland shade of taupe.

You're probably wondering how Beth got involved in all this. She's never been a big tea person like me, but she caught me carting a boatload of cleaning products out of our pantry at home and offered to drive me to the shop with them. I've been so worried that she decided to act like an actual big sister for once and stay to help us. My mom probably made her.

Jonathan talked and talked about "economies of scale" and "appealing to a younger demographic." He seemed to have pages and pages of things to say about profit margins and returns on investment, which I supposed was a good thing. After getting some additional advice from a couple of trusted (grown-up) friends, Louisa decided to get a small business loan through the bank on our street, part of which she also used to pay the back bills from wholesalers.

Anyway, I rewrote the chalkboard menu, taking off over half of the teas and raising all prices by fifteen cents (Jonathan had wanted to jump thirty; Louisa bargained him down). The French soap in the bathroom was replaced—not even with Dial but with a generic brand. Jonathan picked out some copycat chairs online, and when they arrived, sure enough, they were not very comfortable. By Sunday night, the Steeping Leaf looked very different than it had on Friday afternoon. It was modern, clean, and . . . awful. But Jonathan had never been in a better mood since I met him. He walked around with a pleased expression on his face, like he owned the place. And he was more chatty than I'd ever seen him before. Every few minutes he was talking to Beth about this or that.

Louisa seemed to age a bit that weekend. Each item we took out of the shop was like an old friend to her, whether it was a lush houseplant or a variety of tea that hadn't sold in months. She kept touching the things that remained, as if for reassurance. It felt terrible watching her shop disappear, but what choice did we have? Losing the Leaf altogether would be unbearable. The changes had to be worth it. They just had to. And after all, she is the one who always counseled that change was the way of the universe.

While we worked, some neighbors stopped by to see what we were up to, including Mr. Silverman. He watched for a few minutes, and I brought him an iced tea because it was pretty hot outside.

"Thank you for *Mansfield Park*, Mr. Silverman. I've read two chapters already and it is wonderful."

"You're very welcome, Annie. Don't you just love the smell of old books?"

"I do! It is so completely unique."

"Like this furniture," he said, gesturing about. "I remember when your grandfather and Louisa first collected it.

They told everyone on the street what they needed and got first dibs before garage sales began. This couch, in fact, was mine." He chuckled at the well-loved, outdated pattern and patted it affectionately. "Your grandfather planted these bushes over here," he said, gesturing at the lilacs, "and cajoled several of his graduate students into laying these stones," he remembered, resting his elbow on the patio's low surrounding wall. "Charles was the kind of person people just wanted to help out. Gosh, some of those graduate students are probably grandparents themselves now."

I could see that Mr. Silverman loved to remember. Louisa joined us, and they laughed together as Mr. Silverman related a story about my grandfather and his schemes.

"Do you remember when Charles decided to try to host the entire Madison Jazz Orchestra?" Mr. Silverman asked. "It was standing room only, Annie, and just barely. I'd never seen a trombonist smack someone in the head before. Rather entertaining, actually."

"It sure was," Louisa agreed. "Though not in quite the way Charles intended. After that, we made a rule. No more than five musicians inside at one time. Quite the challenge when your mother started bringing her starving band friends in for free biscotti," she said to me. I smiled.

Sometimes I forgot that the Leaf was practically my mom's living room when she was in high school.

Now that I knew my grandmother was back in a good mood, all I had to do was figure out how to have a real date with Jonathan. Working alongside him all weekend was really nice. I finally stopped feeling so awkward, even. Pretending to be braver than I actually was, I followed him out back to help decide what things should be saved and stored and what things should be placed on the curb. I smoothed my shirt, patted down my out-of-control hair, and smiled at him.

"The place looks great. I can't believe we did all that in one weekend."

"I know. I didn't think we could get it done. But we did." He smiled at me with a wink. We both sat down on the curb, taking a much-needed break. Jonathan's knee touched mine and I leaned into his shoulder, grinning. I kept asking myself, *How would Genna handle this?*

"Your shoe's untied," he said. I looked down at it and then at him. It was.

"Why don't you, um. Maybe . . . tie it. For me?" I squeaked. I couldn't believe I could be so flirtatious. It was like another person had momentarily taken over my body.

With a loud sigh and a smirk, Jonathan carefully put my foot in his lap (*gasp!*) and slowly, slowly took all my laces out and then put them back. He tied my shoe. It was, and I am not kidding here, the most romantic thing that ever happened to me. I stopped breathing. He gently placed my foot back on the pavement, then looked at me uncertainly and shook his head a tiny bit. I would have sold my two brothers to know what he was thinking. Suddenly my sister appeared, with the worst timing of anyone in the entire universe.

"What's up, guys?" she asked, sipping on a bottle of water. She was *so* the bottled water type. Ugh.

"Your lil sis can't keep her shoes tied," Jonathan answered, in a tone that clearly said, Isn't she silly and so much younger than us? He stood up quickly and resumed looking at Beth like she was an angel.

"Yeah, Annie's shoes are never tied. Anyway, I think we're done."

The spell—if you could call it that—was broken. I thought I might spontaneously break out in hives right then and there. My favorite place looked so foreign, and the boy I liked appeared to be crushy on my *sister*, of all people. Ew. I mean, he was a sophomore and she was a *senior*. I conveniently forgot that I was an eighth grader. For her part, Beth barely noticed her new fan; she was just happy to be done with the physical labor of the renovation. She wandered back inside and chatted

LAURA SCHAEFER

with Louisa about the college she had selected, and how she couldn't wait to be out on her own. I followed her in. Louisa winked at me, a silent acknowledgment that despite everything, the tea wouldn't change. It was a small comfort. I felt like my aura had dulled.

At lunch period the next day, Genna was lecturing me on how to behave more like a sophisticated high school student, now that middle school was almost done. I can't even begin to deal. I was just starting to feel sort of maybe okay about the whole middle school thing, and now I have to start over again at the bottom in high school. *Ugh.* Anyway, apparently I have to get some sort of "hairstyle" before ninth grade begins in the fall, which Genna does not understand is contrary to the laws of physics. If only she had to walk a day in my frizz.

Genna agreed that the Shoe Episode, as we now called it, was a clear sign that Jonathan was falling in love with me, and it was only a matter of time before we made it official. This, she says, is the key to my success in high school. Arriving with a BF. Apparently it's a guaranteed social in. Okay, I conveniently left out the part of the story where Jonathan followed Beth around like a pathetic puppy dog. At least in Genna's world, a romance between me and hottie Barista Boy was still possible.

The Ten-Step Program
for Becoming a Gorgeous Goddess
by Annie Green and Genna Matthews

1. Brush, floss, and apply tooth whitener every day until teeth look like Chiclets.

2. Do crunches, lunges, and yoga poses four times a week so as to acquire long, lean muscles and gymnastlike flexibility.

3. Eat healthy food like nuts, berries, fish, whole grains, green veggies, yogurt, avocadoes, tomatoes, etc. No more Funyuns!

4. Learn to belly dance.

5. Stop pulling dental floss from nose to mouth to make people laugh at school.

6. Convince parents to pay for subscriptions to at least four respected fashion periodicals.

7. Paint nails more often.

8. Apply mint mask to face to get rid of nature's cruel jokes.

9. Smile mysteriously.

10. Practice Scarlett Johansson–style deep voice.

"I want to see the dental-floss trick again," Zoe said when we presented her with the list. She was eating pizza with a knife and fork, which Genna and I were used to by now. Even when we were little she used a fork to eat the barely bite-sized muffins Louisa made at the Leaf.

"No way. That has been retired." Genna spoke with finality. "Annie never did that anyway. Suburban legend."

"I did so. Sixth-grade spring field trip. But don't worry. I didn't bring any floss to school."

"Good."

"Let's see, I've got pizza, you've got mac and cheese, and is that a taco, Annie?" Zoe was laughing at our weak goddess resolve. The three of us weren't exactly the healthiest eaters. At least Zo also had a sliced apple and a Powerbar before her.

"I didn't say it would happen overnight. You've got to ease into being a goddess." Genna said this like a respected psychiatrist on *Oprah*.

"That's right. Too much healthy food at once would be a shock to my system," I added. And then I smiled mysteriously and pouted my lips.

"You two are crazy. Oh, whoops. I have a tennis thing. We're supposed to be eating together." Zoe grabbed her pizza slice, apple, and Powerbar and sped off. "See yas."

"Oh, yeah. I'm supposed to be helping Miss Keltcher in the art room. I promised I'd clean up at lunch. It was wild times with the pottery wheels today." Genna tossed her mac and cheese into the garbage and smoothed her pencil skirt. "We'll try to make it to the shop later."

"Wait!" I wanted to talk more about the Leaf but didn't know what to say. I knew Gen and Zo wouldn't like the drastic changes we had made. After it was out of my mouth, I tried to think of something to say as Genna paused. "Um, never mind. Have fun getting clay off the ceiling."

When I was done with my taco, I walked up to the front of the cafeteria to clean my tray and Zach tripped me.

"Hey, neighbor," he said with a salute.

"Hey *what*?" I replied, resisting the urge to "accidentally" spill the rest of my milk on him.

"You, me, neighbors. Don'tcha remember, Green? It's official. I'm moving to your street. I know, I know, you're speechless with joy. I'd much rather not live among the plebes, but what can you do? My inheritance hasn't kicked in yet."

"Zach, I am not even dealing with you right now. Stay out of the Leaf." I brushed past him as his friends hooted and laughed.

That's all I needed; for my new best customer to be Zach Anderson.

GENNA'S
TEA GODDESS BEAUTY TIPS

1. RINSE DARK HAIR WITH BLACK TEA ONCE A WEEK TO ADD SHININESS.

2. RINSE LIGHT HAIR WITH CHAMOMILE TEA TO MAKE HIGHLIGHTS DAZZLE-Y.

3. AFTER YOU WASH YOUR FACE, PUT SOME COOL WHITE TEA ONTO A COTTON BALL AND SMOOTH OVER THE SKIN LIKE AN ASTRINGENT TO PREVENT ZITS.

4. IF YOU GET A ZIT ANYWAY, PUT A USED TEA BAG RIGHT ON IT AND HOLD FOR A WHILE. DON'T RINSE OFF THE TEA.

Chapter Eleven

Bring me a cup of tea and the *Times*.
—QUEEN VICTORIA'S FIRST COMMAND
UPON HER ASCENSION TO THE THRONE

To celebrate the changes at the Steeping Leaf, Jonathan printed a banner that said TURNING OVER A NEW LEAF. I looked at it and hoped that today would be the day the shop would actually be busy for once. It was almost a week after all the renovations, scarily close to my eighth-grade graduation at the start of June. I am sad to report there have been no more Shoe Episodes and a tea craze has not swept Madison, Wisconsin. To make matters worse, Zach has come in twice to bother me and threaten to report us to the health department (which is crazy, the health department loves us). At least my grandmother looked happy to see me.

"Hi, Annie."

"Hey, Louisa. How's your day going?"

"Oh, I don't know. I think my planets are out of alignment. The regulars don't like our new shop. Mr. Silverman understands why we made the changes, but when I asked him for an honest opinion, he wrinkled his nose. And I haven't seen Mr. and Mrs. Kopinski or their matching outfits since the day they saw the updates and asked if I'd sold the place. The yoga ladies stopped coming by after their afternoon class, and even the robin seems to have abandoned her nest." Louisa looked very worried.

"They don't like it at all?" I had to admit, I wasn't that surprised.

"No. Or our new prices."

"Yikes." What had we done?

"Oh good, there are Ling and Hieu. I haven't seen them since the teething fit. You want to go open the door for her, dear?" Ling was pushing the stroller and Hieu was actually smiling. I opened the door so Ling could leave him buckled in.

"Hi there, Ling. How are you?" She looked much better, rested even.

"Good afternoon, Annie. Thanks. I'm doing well, how are you?"

"I'm good." I saw Ling notice the changes in the shop, taking everything in slowly. "Am I in the right store?"

"Yes. We did a little, ah, remodeling last weekend."

"I see that. Wow." She parked the stroller by the counter and looked around. "Hi there, Louisa."

"Ling, hello. How did the herbs work out?"

"Oh, perfectly. Thank you so much. Hieu is practically a different child. Well, this week anyway. I've started bracing for the terrible twos. I sure hope there is an herb for those!" Louisa and Ling laughed knowingly together, but I couldn't help noticing that Ling hadn't said anything at all about the new paint and furniture. I wondered if she was sticking to the old *If you can't say anything nice, don't saying anything at all* rule. I decided not to ask. Instead, I prepared Ling's cucumber sandwich order so she could chat with Louisa about their respective gardens. It was almost time to plant tomatoes, apparently.

After Ling and Hieu left, I asked Louisa if she had said anything about the "New Leaf."

"Well, not exactly. Just that she was glad we hadn't changed the cucumber sandwiches at all."

"Hmm," was all I said in reply. I guess I wasn't the only one in the world who wasn't fond of changes.

"Annie, love, I think I'm going to go over a few things in back. Are you all right handling the counter on your own?"

"Sure."

Louisa went back into the storeroom. Today, I was supposed to be working with Jonathan, but after he arrived, he kept disappearing into the back room to make our inventory "more efficient." I was spending more time daydreaming about him than actually talking to him. He seemed even more distant than usual. Guys were impossible to understand. I could tell that he was disappointed. The New Leaf scheme wasn't turning into the business miracle he thought it would.

Just as I was about to say something brilliant (or as close to brilliant as was possible under the circumstances, like, "I see you like milk in your tea"), he went and clocked out, grumbling about the slow customer traffic.

The shop was in its typical late-afternoon quiet time, which seemed worse now that there weren't even any houseplants to talk to. I straightened the tables and made sure everything was fully stocked. Since I was allowed to study, I pulled out my science book to review for our test on plate tectonics. It was actually kind of a cool chapter; I know, I am a total nerd. I was almost done going over the chapter review section when Genna and Zoe came in. I grinned at them.

Genna was dressed in tight jeans and red shoes that

buckled over her ankle. An orange newsboy cap sat on her head, and she had her art portfolio under her arm. Zoe looked comfortable in white shorts and Pumas, her long black hair smooth behind a headband. It was tough having such gorgeous friends when I was stuck in my barista apron. "Teashop Girls reunion!" Genna shouted, taking her place center stage as usual.

"Okay, we went weeks without bugging you at work," Zoe announced, a little apologetically. "Now I want to see if you can really make that time machine thingy work." She pointed her finger at the chrome espresso machine.

"I am the espresso wizard. We're pals, he and I." I patted the machine with affection and leaned on the counter in front of my friends. We were, at the moment, the only three people in the store.

"Okay, I know it's been a while, but what happened to this place? It looks so different." Zoe touched the empty shelves and plopped herself into one of the uncomfortable chairs and made a face. I remembered the three of us in the old chairs, our feet not even close to the ground. Louisa had always been careful to make us the mild tea in those days, only steeping it a bit and adding lots of cream and sugar. I wondered if she still had some of those miniature tea sets around.

"Yeah, it was Jonathan's idea. He said we had to join the twenty-first century."

"Seriously? This?" she said, gesturing. "And you *want* him? Why?"

"Did you, like, lock the door or something?" Genna looked around. "It's deserted."

"No, but I should've." I put away my homework; it was a lost cause now. Genna didn't believe in homework, and Zoe always did hers in study hall or late at night when normal, nonsuperheroes were sleeping. "What can I get for you?"

"*What can I get for you?* Aww, you sound just like a pro!"

"Yeah . . ." I totally did. I smiled.

"Um, how about some of that red tea to match my shoes. You like?" Genna stuck her foot up near the counter. Zoe held out an arm to steady her.

"Gen, I swear you are going to break something." Zoe turned to me. "I'll take an English breakfast."

"'Kay." I poured the drinks and leaned against the counter while Gen and Zo sat.

"I forgot how much I missed this place. Remember when I tried to catch a lightning bug out front when we were ten?"

"You were trying to impress some dumb boy," Zoe

reminded her. "And almost mushed the poor thing. Gross." It was true. I laughed. I was glad that had been Genna's first and last experiment with the area wildlife.

"Speaking of dumb guys, ask Venus Williams here what happened at tennis practice." Genna sipped her tea and gestured to Zoe. "But wait, where is your guy? I thought the whole reason you loved this job was because you could breathe the same air as Barista Boy all day."

"That is *not* the whole reason. I'm helping my grandmother."

"Right."

"Well, he isn't here that much as it turns out. I guess he must have a paper due or something. We've exchanged about three meaningful sentences since the Shoe Episode. You think I should wear something, you know, cuter?"

"Yes," Genna said.

"No," Zoe replied at exactly the same time.

"Anyway, what happened to you today at tennis?" I changed the subject. It was pointless to talk about Jonathan since there had been exactly zero developments in that department and whenever I did see him, he steered the conversation to Beth. Ugh. Zoe looked embarrassed at the question, which was weird.

"All right. You know we had that pretournament

scrimmage today? Ugh, this chair sucks." Zoe shifted in the hard chair and glared at it. "Anyway, the guys' tennis team against the girls'? I had to play Zach Anderson, of course."

"Mmm, icky." Zach deserved to have his butt handed to him. Zoe was perfectly capable of doing it, too, so I was wondering why she looked so miserable.

"Yeah. Anyway, in the middle of the second set, he starts with the foot faults. We didn't have a line judge because it was a scrimmage. I called him on some of them, and he said I was just worried he was going to win. I tried to ignore him, but he just kept pushing me and pushing me. So I nailed him with a serve when he wasn't looking. Of course, that's the moment when his coach walks over. Zach whined so loud about how much it hurt and how he was calling his dad's lawyer that my coach had to agree to take me off the roster for the tournament. So now some poor bench sitter has to play number one singles. I'm an idiot." Zoe sucked on her drink. "My stepdad is going to be so mad at me. I think I'm getting a stomachache."

"Not fair! He was asking for it."

"I know. He totally was. But I have to learn to control my temper. So says my coach. She is *peeved*." Zoe looked down and started picking at the skin around her fingernails, which was raw.

"But your coach doesn't have to put up with Zach on a daily basis. Half the school must've cheered when you clocked him." I was upset. The tournament was a big deal. Zoe had been talking about it for two weeks. Last year, she lost in the final round and felt this was the chance to go all the way. Zach should've been supportive; Zoe represented his school and his tennis program. There was no reason for him to cheat. What a jerk.

"Yeah. But there isn't much I can do about it now."

"We could egg his house," Genna offered.

"Nah. That wouldn't get me in the match." Zoe looked defeated. Her thumb was starting to bleed from all the picking.

"But *I'd* feel better," Genna said.

"We need to fix this; it isn't right. TSGs do not get pushed around." I couldn't stand to see Zoe so bummed out. "Zach should go to the coaches and explain what happened. I'm sure if you apologized to him, they'd figure something out." I chewed on a pencil, trying to figure out how best to butter him up.

"Uh-oh, you've awakened the little Wonder Barista," Genna said. "Annie, why don't you pay off the national debt and solve global warming while you're at it?"

"Ha-ha."

Genna started pulling out her artwork. "You think

Louisa would let me hang some of these up? You know, like, for sale?"

"Gen, since when is a picture of your thumb *art*?" Zoe peered at the first drawing. I grinned. I never really "got" Genna's more conceptual art, just as I never understood why we had to start school at 7:35 a.m. Or why some women got eyeliner tattooed permanently on their faces.

"Um, hello. Since I painted the nail with a pagoda. See?"

"You think someone is going to buy that?"

"Sure. It's original. And look how detailed!"

"Uh-uh. I'm sure some Madison art-buyer is just dying to hang up a picture of your big thumb in their living room."

"They totally are. Anyway, back to Zach. How do we punish him?" Genna looked at me expectantly.

"Well, we could make a gift of a certain thumb drawing . . ." Zoe offered as I giggled. Genna stuck out her tongue. "Aww, we like your pictures, Gen. Just put them here and I'll ask Louisa later. As for Zach, we definitely need a list." I flipped over the blackboard listing the tea of the day to reveal the whiteboard on the back and eagerly uncapped my dry-erase marker.

"Uh-oh, Louisa lets you have access to a whiteboard and dry-erase marker? How many lists have you made since you started?" Zoe demanded.

"Oh, one or two a day. I'm trying to limit myself. But Louisa says she's never been so on top of inventory. All right. Here we go. MAKING ZACH ANDERSON SORRY HE IS ALIVE AND/OR GETTING ZOE BACK INTO TOURNAMENT." I started writing superfast as Genna gave suggestions.

1. Put a few sushi rolls deep in his locker.

"Genna!" Zoe said, aghast. "We just figured out about the moldy subs; obviously the boy is hard of smelling."

"Hey, she wrote it down."

"We are in a brainstorming phase," I said. "Seriously, though. Less grossness, Genna."

"Whatever."

2. Circulate a petition to reinstate Zoe.

"Annie, you circulate a petition every other week. I think people are getting tired of it."

"They are not."

3. Bribe him with homework answers.
4. Stage a school walkout in protest of Zoe's punishment.
5. Cast a voodoo spell on him.

6. *Start a rumor that he still sleeps with his blankie.*

"Harsh, Gen."

"It would totally work."

"Maybe." Zoe slurped up the rest of her drink and leaned back in her chair. "Anyway, we're not going to do anything. The point is, I already nailed Zach in the head for playing like a weasel. I even messed up his stupid faux-hawk. So we better let it rest or I'll be out for the rest of the season."

"That's so mature of you, it makes me sick," Genna said, disgusted.

"Eh, a couple of the players have already decided to TP his house this weekend after the tourney," Zoe added sheepishly.

"Awesome! You want to help them, Annie? Annie?" Genna spun around in her chair to see Jonathan enter the shop. I was nonchalantly flipping the board back over. I figured my One True Love didn't need to know that I was fond of circulating petitions through my school or capable of bribery.

"Hey, Jonathan. These are my friends."

"Annie, what's up? I forgot my math book." I made the introductions and saw that Gen looked impressed with

Jonathan's hotness. He looked even cuter than usual because it was a humid day and it made his hair stick to the back of his neck a bit.

"So I heard all this new furniture was your idea." Zoe looked at Jonathan with an annoyed expression on her face. I bit my lip.

"Yup. What do you think?"

"Sucks. I liked the old stuff." Sometimes I wished I could be as certain as Zoe. She didn't wait for other people to give an opinion before agreeing with it. She just said what she thought. I sent her positive mental waves.

"Well, come in and spend five hundred bucks a day and I'll get it back for you."

"Right. I can see your new decorating is bringing in *swarms* of new customers," Zoe shot back. Jonathan sighed and slumped onto a stool at the counter.

"Yeah, it's not good. One more month of days like this and Annie and I will no longer have jobs."

"It's not that bad is it? This place has been around longer than *I* have." To Genna, that meant it was somehow permanent. Zoe sat up, looking concerned.

"Yeah. It *is* that bad. But don't worry, with our experience I'm sure Annie and I can always get a job across the street." He patted my shoulder, but I didn't even feel a single stomach butterfly. "Anyway, is Louisa still here?"

"Um, yeah, in the back," I said, distracted. Jonathan disappeared.

"I don't know, Annie," Zoe said. "He's kind of a jerk."

"Sheesh," Genna agreed. "You're right, though. Major yum."

"Annie, stop looking like your dog just died," Zoe urged. "I'm sure it's not that bad." I fiddled with my hair, wishing Zoe was right.

"Do you see how bummed I look? We have *got* to do something else."

"Like what?"

"I don't know. Whatever Meg Ryan did in *You've Got Mail!*"

"Didn't the store close at the end of the movie?" Zoe asked.

"Okay, whatever she did, but better! You see, Jonathan thought he could save this place by making it more like . . ." I jerked my thumb toward the opposite side of the street. "But we know what it's *really* about."

"You are one gosh-darn chipper girl, Annie Meghan Green. How have I put up with you all these years?" Genna smiled and started placing her artwork around the shop. "Not to sound like Ms. Doomsday, but don't you think it might be tough to pass eighth grade, do all your chores, make Zach Anderson sorry he was born, *and* save the Leaf? Especially since your OCD demands that you write nine amusing lists per day?"

"No."

"Oh, God," Zoe muttered. "I can see the wheels turning. You think you can make Jonathan fall in love with you if you somehow manage to single-handedly get a bunch of customers in here."

"Not single-handedly."

"Is this where we all put our hands in the center of the circle and shout 'Teashop Girls Power!'?"

"Yes."

I looked at my two best friends expectantly, who nodded and bounced out of their chairs. Gen and Zo gave me their pinkies and we all solemnly shook.

During World War II, my great-grandmother Cecilia worked long hours in a factory doing her part for the war effort. When she got home in the evening she'd always make herself a cup of tea to relax and a little cup for Louisa as well. It was their special tradition and now it's ours.

Chapter Twelve

If this is coffee, please bring me some tea;
but if this is tea, please bring me coffee.
—ABRAHAM LINCOLN

The New Leaf of Jonathan's dreams was a dismal failure. There was no other word for it. Business was slumping even more than it had been when I was first hired. Louisa was forced to close the shop even earlier because it was so expensive to run all the lights and the monster espresso machine. The owner of the building served the Leaf a new eviction notice, which gave us three weeks to clear out in the event of another late payment of rent.

I was never on the schedule at the same time as Jonathan because it was clear there weren't enough customers for two baristas. Regardless, I refused to get too upset. Genna and Zoe had promised they would do whatever I wanted in order to save the shop. The Teashop Girls could not, *would not* fail.

Top Ten Eleven Ways the Teashop Girls Will Save the Steeping Leaf and Put a Certain Demonic Coffee Chain Out of Business, or at Least the Monroe Street Location

1. Hold more events:
   Poetry readings
   Book signings
   Open-mike night
   Cooking classes
   Herbal remedy classes
   Matchmaking night for single people
   Afternoon tea, like they have at the Plaza,
      by reservation only

2. Print up pretty fliers designed by Genna and staple them around the university.

3. Get the local media to feature the place . . . *as it was*.

4. Hold a grand thirtieth-anniversary celebration for all the neighbors and regulars.

5. Put coupons in the student papers and hand out

yummy samples all over town.

6. Stage a demonstration in front of competitor.
7. Get all friends at school and their families to boycott competitor.
8. Get more varieties of tea, not fewer.
9. Find a way to emit the smell of freshly baked scones into the street.
10. Bring back French soaps . . . _sell_ French soaps!
11. Pair up with spas for cross-promotion.

I was proud of my work. It had taken me two whole days of thinking to put the list together. I even talked to my dad. He looked happy to be asked about a problem he understood, instead of the usual daughter dramas involving unruly red hair. He gently reminded me, however, that no matter how much the Teashop Girls managed to increase business in the next few weeks, an eviction notice was very serious. As if I didn't know. As it turned out, my mother and he had spent several long hours going over their finances, trying to figure out a way to buy Louisa's building, but they just couldn't find a way to afford it. I think they've already been helping with a portion of the rent and my mom's practical side won't let that go on much longer. In her opinion, Louisa should probably retire.

I had only an hour left of my shift before closing time and was thinking about Jonathan's reaction when he learned that the shop had become a multimillion-dollar empire. He would have to admit he was wrong about the whole French soap thing and retie *both* my shoes, and then who knows . . . Beth would be leaving for college, after all. I planned to talk to Louisa about it while we were cleaning up. My grandmother was on the phone in back, trying to negotiate with some suppliers.

She emerged from her office and turned to me, looking less than centered.

"It is hard to practice loving-kindness with wholesalers, my sweetness. It's like they're doing me a favor, selling me their products. And the prices! You would think these tea leaves were made of pure gold. They're really pushing those pyramid shaped teabags, but you know how I feel about those, dear." I did. Some tea drinkers liked the three-dimensional nylon bags because they allowed more room for the tea to expand. But Louisa would never use them because the synthetic nylon wasn't good for the environment.

"I'm sorry, Louisa. Listen, I don't know if this is a good time or not, but I've been thinking about a couple new ways to drum up some more business."

"Oh goodness, not you too. I suppose you want me to get all matching mugs or something."

"No, no, nothing like that. I think we should make the Steeping Leaf like it was . . . only better. Genna and Zoe and I want to make sure it's still here when *we* have Teashop Girls of our own."

"I'm listening . . ."

I flipped over the board and proudly displayed my list. I offered to work on planning events during my normal shifts between serving customers. It wasn't going to be difficult, since I probably make only a handful of drinks each hour. Louisa couldn't help but be impressed. Which was a good thing, because I already e-mailed every feature writer in the city I could find, and one of them was showing up in five minutes to interview Louisa about her shop.

"Well, Annie dear, everything looks pretty interesting." Louisa smiled. "Do you really want to do the extra work?"

"Oh, yes. This place means a lot to me. I'll submit everything for your approval before I go too crazy. I promise. Oh! And I want to call about maybe getting this building registered as an official historical place."

"All right, then. Carry on, love. You've got spunk."

"I'm very glad you feel that way, because Ally Livingston from the *Isthmus* is going to be here in about two minutes to interview you."

"Annie!"

"What? It'll be good. She said she had a piece fall

apart at the last minute, so she's going to put us in this week's issue!"

Louisa looked slightly dazed for a minute and then recovered, quickly surveying the store to see that everything was in place. I straightened out my apron and grinned.

"What are these?" Louisa gestured to Genna's prints, which were resting against the back of the counter.

"Oh, I almost forgot. Genna wants to know if you'd be interested in taking these on, um, consignment? She's an aspiring artist, you know. She said to tell you that her influences are, um, Andy Warhol, Rene Magritte, and Annie Lebowitz? Does that sound right? If you don't like them, it's okay."

"No, they're fun. I'll put them over here. The walls are so bare; it's making me nervous anyway. Tell Genna thank you for me."

The shop door jingled and a woman with a camera stepped over the threshold. I ran up to greet her, trying not to bounce too much.

"Ms. Livingston? I'm Annie Green."

"Nice to meet you."

"And this is Louisa Shanahan. We're so happy you're here."

Here is a sketch Genna drew of our tea counter at the Leaf. It shows some of our many tea varieties and a triple layer cake minus the hearty piece Louisa and I ate. If only we could get her to do more drawings like this and less thumb art . . .

Chapter Thirteen

A Proper Tea is much nicer than a Very Nearly Tea,
which is one you forget about afterwards.

—A. A. MILNE

I wandered home, sorry to be leaving the shop, but I had my tea paper to finish and, I was freaking out because I had waited until the last possible moment. Breathe in. Breathe out. Breathe in. . . . I tried to think some calming thoughts. It could be worse. Everything was going to be okay. I could do the writing before bedtime and wake up a little early tomorrow before school and print it out. I already had a topic, an outline, *and* a rough draft, after all. I remembered that I wanted to add some things: June is National Iced Tea Month (how cool is that?), and there was once talk in Washington, DC, back in the 1920s, of making tea the national beverage. I walked through my front door just as the phone was ringing. Billy picked it up, still in a trance from his video game.

"'Lo? . . . Yeah. Hey. No, she's gone. I dunno."

"Billy! I'm here." I rushed to the phone. "Hello?"

"It's me," Zoe's voice announced. "What are you doing?"

"I have to write a paper. It's due first period."

"Oh. Well, you can stay up late, I do it all time. I got us in at Samadhi Spa!"

"What?"

"You know, to help promote the shop!"

"Wow, that was fast. Fantastic, Zo."

"My mom is friends with the owner. She says she's really nice and definitely wants to meet us. Genna said she'd do the talking. Meet up at my place?"

"Okay, sounds good. I just have to change clothes."

"'Kay." We hung up and I went to my room, rummaged through my closet to find some nice clothes, and changed. Thank goodness my parents were at a concert. Wait, that meant Beth was in charge. Horrors. I put my hair into a ponytail and knocked on my sister's door.

"Hey," I said. Dear sis looked up uninterestedly from her issue of *Vanity Fair*.

"What's with you?" Beth gestured to the dressy outfit.

"Oh, it's for the Leaf. I have to go back to work." Well, in a way.

"Whatever." My sister didn't even question it. "It's your turn to empty the dishwasher and clean out Truman's cat box."

"Okay."

I hurried over to Zoe's place and met her and Genna. Both of them looked very determined; I was so sure nothing could stop us . . . not even rain this time. We all headed down to the shopping area near the Leaf on our bikes, talking all the way about how the Samadhi Spa could help our cause.

"I bet they could use Louisa's tea in their waiting room!" Genna cried, gesturing so much she almost fell off her pink vintage cruiser.

"Or in their skin treatments," Zoe agreed. She carefully steered around a pothole. "A tea facial. Or a tea bath!"

"Mmm, sounds nice," I said. I'd never been to a spa, but I could imagine how fun it would be to have good-smelling things rubbed on my face. I carried the Handbook with me just in case, and it turned out to be a good thing. Genna wanted to take a look at the "Health Benefits of Tea" page. She's hoping to turn it into posters made of rice paper from the art studio at school and have it proudly displayed at lots of places like Samadhi Spa. I just hoped the owner there would steer customers in our direction. After all, they were a local business too. I was sure we could help each other.

We arrived at the spa just as the sun was starting to set. The orange light filled the tranquil front room, and I breathed in its perfumed air. A receptionist with stick-straight hair welcomed us. The place was super fancy. I was impressed. All the furniture was low and plain but looked very expensive. There were a few white candles arranged on the tabletops, and a large bamboo tree in the corner. On the front desk sat a bonsai plant. Genna, armed with the Handbook for courage, stepped forward and was shown to another room to meet with Samadhi's owner. I was so glad she had volunteered to talk. I would have been so scared.

Zoe and I sat in the waiting area and were quiet for several minutes. It just seemed like the kind of place you weren't supposed to talk much. We stared at a small waterfall trickling near the front desk. Finally, Zoe leaned over to me to whisper.

"What do you think she's saying in there?" she asked.

"I don't know." Then I said, "Well, I'm sure she's explaining the Leaf's troubles and hopefully getting the Samadhi Spa to help. Don't you think it would be nice to have afternoon tea after a massage or whatever?" I wasn't sure exactly what went on in spas, but I was pretty sure a massage was part of the deal.

"Definitely. Annie? I have a question for you." Zoe looked hesitant, which was unlike her. Usually she looked like she was on her way to take over a small nation.

"Okay, what is it?"

"Well, you know how I hit Zach with a serve?"

"Sure, I think it's awesome," I replied.

"I know, everyone does. But it bothers me. I've never totally lost it like that on the court before. I was so angry," she said.

"We understand, Zo. Anyone would be."

"Maybe. But the thing is, I don't really want to be like that. I know my parents disagree, but it really is just a game." I thought about Zoe's parents for a minute. They usually seemed mad about something. I guess I was pretty lucky to have a mom and dad like mine. "Anyway, remember when Louisa used to talk to us about monks in Japan? How peaceful they are? I want to be more like them."

"You do?" I wondered if any monks had ever won a tennis match.

"Yes, I do. So . . . I was thinking maybe Louisa could give us, like, a meditation lesson." She picked at her fingernail and looked at me. I was surprised. Zoe was so practical and scientific about things that it seemed odd she wanted to learn how to think about nothing. But that's just what she seemed to want. I was kind of happy for her. I knew Louisa would enjoy teaching the practice of meditation. She had meditated every day for many, many years. I believe my grandfather had done it as well, often right out on the patio at the Leaf.

"I'm sure she would be happy to, Zo. Why don't you come by the shop tomorrow after practice?" I offered.

"Okay, I will."

Genna came out then and gave us the thumbs-up. We shook hands with the owner lady and were on our way. On the ride home, we interrogated Gen.

"Sooooo? What did she say?" Zoe asked.

"She was really nice," Genna said, drawing out the suspense. "She said that she would be happy to hand out tea samples and include an afternoon tea at the Leaf as part of some of her packages."

"Yes!" I whooped, clapping and almost falling off my bike. "Good job, Gen."

"Yeah, totally," agreed Zoe. We all smiled as Genna continued.

"She'll be calling Louisa tomorrow morning to work out all the details." Gen paused, thoughtful. "I'm going to also talk to the people at my theater, and see if maybe they'd give us a deal on advertising both the teashop and the spa in the *Much Ado About Nothing* playbills."

"All right!" I said, my perfect level of cheer returning. It was great news. All we needed to do was stick together, and the shop would be saved. I could feel it.

EVEN <u>MORE</u> OF
GENNA'S TEA GODDESS BEAUTY TIPS

1. USE COLD, USED TEA BAGS AS EYE COMPRESSES. VERY SPA-Y AND RELAXING.

2. DRINK GREEN TEA BECAUSE IT IS GOOD FOR YOU, AND HEALTHY PEOPLE ARE GORGEOUS!

3. MAKE A FACIAL SCRUBBING MASK WITH CORNMEAL, MILK, AND CHAMOMILE TEA. JUST MAKE SURE YOU AREN'T AROUND ANNIE'S LIVING ROOM WHEN YOU PUT IT ON, OR HER DOG WILL TRY TO LICK IT OFF BEFORE IT HAS A CHANCE TO DRY.

4. IF YOU HAVE A SUNBURN, PUT ABOUT SIX BLACK TEA BAGS IN YOUR BATHTUB. STEEP IN THERE ALONG WITH THE TEA FOR ABOUT TEN MINUTES. IT REALLY HELPS!

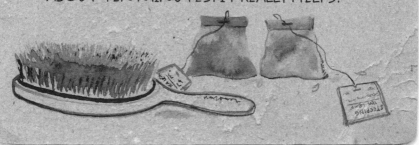

Chapter Fourteen

Thank God for tea! What would the world do without tea?
How did it exist? I am glad I was not born before tea.

—SYDNEY SMITH

Zach Anderson came up behind me right before the last bell of the day rang. I jumped out of the way and glared at him.

"Hey, Teashop Girl, you know anything about the *decorations* in my yard?"

"What?"

I suddenly remembered what Zoe had said about her teammates' plans to toilet-paper his house, but I met Zach's gaze looking all confused. Genna wasn't the *only* actress around, apparently.

"Oh, I'm sure you know nothing about it, since you are too busy trying to beg people to come to your grandma's shop."

"Go away, you mutant."

"Tell your friend Zoe she's got a weak backhand."

"She'd kill you on the court anytime and you know it. Are we done here?" I pushed past him and walked out. I was so wrapped up in sending negative vibes to Zach that I jumped when Genna appeared and put her arm around me.

"I've been thinking about Operation Save the Leaf Phase Three," she said.

"Me too. It's practically all I *can* think about." I sighed. "Louisa says thanks, by the way, for the Samadhi Spa visit. I guess that's working out pretty well." I didn't mention that the shop was still *reeeaaally* slow.

"Cool. Anyway, here's the thing. We have to get the people here at school into the Leaf. You know?"

"I do know. How?" I'd been wondering the same thing. It was so difficult, though, to convince kids to try something new. "I think it'll be pretty tough to convince everyone that tea is, um, cool."

"Yeah. But maybe we could hand out samples and coupons and stuff." Genna had a serious expression on her face.

"That could work . . ." I smiled. It was *something*.

"See, there's this rumor that Zach's dad wants to buy up property in Vilas for a new condo development. I'm really worried," Genna said, a panicked expression on her face. Her parents knew all the Madison muckety-mucks, including the Andersons. I frowned.

"Oh man, it's true," I said, my heart sinking. "Zach was on my street and has been making all these noises about moving to our neighborhood."

"Ugh," Genna was uncharacteristically taciturn.

It hadn't occurred to me when I talked to Zach during my reconnaissance mission with Jonathan that Mr. Anderson might want to get his Condo King hands on Louisa's shop. It felt like we were racing against a clock to save what might be unsavable. If Mr. Anderson was anything like his son, he wasn't going to care one hoot about Louisa and her store . . . even if she had been there for eons. I felt awful, like we were just fighting something much bigger than ourselves. Zoe joined Genna and me in the courtyard. She was carrying her racket, breathless because she was a bit late for practice.

"What up?" Zoe asked.

"Genna's figuring out how to brainwash the school into spending its allowance on tea," I said, a ball of worry about the Andersons and their plans. "We've got to act fast."

"Yes, and you're going to help," Genna added.

"Okay. See you girls lay-ta." Zoe jogged off in a different direction. "I'll call you after practice about coming by the Leaf," she called to me. Genna turned back to me, looking very intense.

"Grab a couple of extra Leaf aprons tonight, and as much tea as you can. Tomorrow is going to be treat day."

"You want to hand out samples?"

"Sure. Supply and demand, baby! You get the supply, I'll create the demand."

Nestea introduced instant tea in 1948, when lots of companies were inventing new "faster" foods, like cake mixes and frozen orange juice. After 1956, instant iced tea drinkers didn't even have to boil water, so the instant stuff became very well-loved, and tea companies were able to compete with soda makers. I dunno, though, I'm still partial to taking my time when it comes to tea. . . .

Chapter Fifteen

Drink your tea slowly and reverently, as if it is the axis on which the world earth revolves—slowly, evenly, without rushing toward the future.

—THICH NHAT HAHN

I was very hopeful about Operation Save the Leaf Phase Three. It felt good to be back in action with Gen and Zo. I headed directly from school to the Steeping Leaf on my bike and talked to Louisa about what brands of tea the shop could spare. There were a couple of pounds of delicious ginger peach that were getting close to the end of their shelf life, so Louisa agreed that it would make the perfect sample. She suggested I print up a hundred sheets of coupons to hand out. I sat in the shop cutting the sheets into fourths and humming to myself. Louisa was busy hanging all of her old posters back up and replacing the big tea bins with her beloved multicolored jars. Jonathan confessed he'd been wrong about the corporate imitation. He sheepishly helped me put back the French soaps.

The Steeping Leaf was starting to look more like itself again. The *Isthmus* reporter Louisa had talked to the other day was sending a photographer for a second story, and they were even thinking about running a short sidebar about brewing the perfect cup of tea. The neighborhood was starting to warm up to the Leaf again. The Kopinskis and their matching outfits were back, several times a week. If only we could hold off the eviction for another month or two . . .

A grumpy customer came in, obviously in a big hurry.

"Can I help you, sir?" I quickly put down the coupon sheets and gave the man my full attention.

"I'll take a triple-shot espresso."

"I'll get that for you right away." I hurried off; he seemed the impatient type. Louisa helped me and handed the man his order.

"Here you go, sir. I took the liberty of putting it in a to-go cup." He gulped it and retreated to a table in the corner, where he looked over the shop appraisingly. He seemed to be doing measurements with his eyes.

"What's with him?"

"I'm not sure. He has come in only once before with

his son, right after you started working, I believe. I think his name is Jeff Anderson. I tried to chat with him, but he isn't all that talkative."

"Mr. Anderson? Was his son my age?"

"Why yes, as a matter of fact."

I looked at Mr. Anderson fearfully. What did he want with the Steeping Leaf? Was he checking out buildings to buy and bulldoze?

I called home to let my mom know I wanted to stay at the shop a bit later than normal and wasn't surprised to see her pop into the shop ten minutes later with Billy in tow. She liked to check up on me when I made myself scarce around the house. They ordered a pot of green tea.

"Hey, Mom, what's up?" I greeted her. Billy and my mom parked at a big table. Billy looked unhappy.

"I decided this one has forgotten what the real world looks like," my mother replied. "He plays the guitar game like his life depends on it."

"Mom!" Billy said. "I want to go home."

"Drink your tea and look at the people for a minute. Your eyes have started to bug out," she answered. I snickered.

"How was work?" I asked my mom.

"Oh, aside from the fact that our best jazz band's rendition of *Stormy Weather* sounds like a pack of cats dying, it was good." She was tough; I knew for a fact that the university's best jazz band was beyond amazing. "How was your day, honey?"

"Fine. Genna and Zoe are going to help me hand out tea samples at school tomorrow."

"That sounds nice, pumpkin. I heard it's going to be rainy."

"Awesome!" There was simply nothing better than a sip of tea on a rainy day.

"Do you have cups?" my mom asked. She was the master of practicality. Four kids will do that to a person, I guess.

"I didn't think of that. Hmm. Can we stop at Target tonight?"

"I think we have some at home, left over from when the paper outlet closed."

"Aren't they, like, three years old?" I wrinkled my nose.

"Paper cups don't expire, Annie."

"Thanks, *Mom*." I smiled. Louisa came over and sat down to chat with us. She hugged my mom and settled into a chair. Billy kept sighing loudly and letting his jaw go slack, his favorite expression.

I danced around in a good mood. The Teashop Girls were finally mobilized, the shop had four customers (okay, two were immediate family, but they *had* left a generous tip in the jar), and when Jonathan learned about everything we were doing to save the shop, he would be so impressed with me that I was sure we'd have another romantic shoe-tying moment. He was in the back, filling out a reorder sheet. When he came out, I decided to explain to him our Operation Save the Leaf.

"So my friends and I are going to hand out Steeping Leaf samples and coupons at school tomorrow," I said. Jonathan was off the clock and busy spreading out his homework at the largest table.

"Good idea," he said simply. I could see him smile a little. It was *so* cute.

"Yeah. Thanks. So . . ." I didn't know what else to say. I wasn't usually this quiet, but with Jonathan it was impossible. If only I was a little older, maybe we'd have more in common. Maybe he'd want to talk to me too. I spent the next twenty minutes paging listlessly through my science book and staring in Jonathan's direction. He was intent on his schoolwork and didn't once start talking to me again. My good mood fizzled out.

Fortunately, Zoe came in then, just as my mom herded my brother out the door. Even in her signature crisp white clothing she looked a little worn out from practice, and she slouched a bit in her chair. I got her a teapot and went to look for Louisa. She hung up the phone and followed me back into the shop, scarf flowing behind her.

"Good evening, dear," Louisa greeted Zoe. They hugged

and, between sips of her tea, Zoe explained why she wanted to learn to meditate. I listened while I cleaned up some tables and straightened the chairs. I heard Louisa explain some things about the practice to my friend. "Meditation will probably not be something you're immediately good at," she explained. "Just like your backhand, it takes years. But the nice thing is, there is immediate benefit." Louisa paused and Zoe nodded. "I want you to think for a minute about what your mind is doing when you're playing a really good match out on the court."

"Okay," Zoe said.

"What is your brain doing when you react to each shot?" Louisa asked. She was so amazing. I appreciated how she could put what she wanted to say in words that made sense to her listener.

"I'm—I'm not really sure," Zoe replied. She looked confused, trying to remember her last good tennis match. Since I finished with my cleanup, I sat down with them. Louisa turned a bit to welcome me to the table, and Zo offered me some of her tea.

"Does your mind tell you where to put your racket each time? Or what step to take?" Louisa said.

"I suppose in a way it does"—Zoe nodded—"but it doesn't feel like it. It almost feels like my mind isn't really there."

"Exactly," replied Louisa. "Piano players often say the same thing. It's like their brain turns off and their fingers know the music."

"Right! I think Genna said that happens sometimes when she draws, too," Zoe remembered.

"And how do you feel when this happens? Does it bother you when your mind turns off like that?"

"Not at all! I love it, actually," said Zoe. "I think it's one reason I play every day. It's, like, peaceful. Well, I mean, when I get in that zone it is. Not when I'm playing with Zach."

"Of course not. The zone, as you say, can be interrupted. The reason I'm bringing this up is it is very relevant to meditation. What is happening to you on the court is a form of meditation, in fact," Louisa said. I looked at her in wonder. I never thought of it that way before. I always thought of meditation as sitting still on a pillow and being calm, something I was terrible at. I wondered what I could do that would put me in a "zone" like Zoe. I didn't play sports or draw or even play piano.

"Cool," Zoe said. "I didn't know that."

"The thing you want to do," Louisa said, "is feel that sort of way at other times. Get into that state off the court. There are many different ways to do it, but the one thing they have in common is the calming of the mind. Almost turning it off. Some people say that praying is talking to God, while meditation is listening to God. It's not the absence of thought, but instead watching thoughts go by. Today, I want us to try first a walking meditation." She rose from our table and showed Zoe and me how to walk mindfully, with a small heel-toe step. Each foot was set directly in front of the other. Louisa motioned for us to try it. We did, but I was having a hard time keeping my mind quiet. There was just so much to think about these days. Zoe seemed to be doing better.

"Good, girls. Excellent. Of course, it is up to you to refocus your minds as they stray. Try to let thoughts go by without becoming attached to them. Just watch what your mind does."

We walked some more and eventually returned to the table. Louisa refilled the teapot and smiled at us.

"But is that really all?" Zoe said. "I didn't feel the same way I did on the court. I kept thinking about a homework assignment."

"It takes time, dear. Some people have a phrase, or mantra, that they say over and over to quiet their minds. You could try that. Some repeat a sound. Others stare at a candle flame, but I've never done that one myself. A sitting meditation might be better for you. Let's try that one." Louisa disappeared into the back for a minute and returned with two square pillows. She placed them on the floor and instructed us in how to sit on them, with our backs very straight and our legs in the lotus pose. "This is my preferred way. Just taking twenty minutes per day to sit and quiet the mind is a powerful thing. One teacher of mine compared our normal state of mind to that of an unmanned fire hose, flipping around." I giggled, remembering such an image from the cartoons. Louisa grinned at me. "To meditate is to bring the fire hose under control so the power of your mind can be used to do great things."

"Wow," Zoe said.

"Indeed. Okay, ladies. I think that about does it for our first lesson." Louisa stood and I knew it was time to start my closing duties. Zoe finished her tea and thanked my grandmother. I could see she had taken the lesson seriously, probably much more than I had. She waved on her way out of the store, a new bounce in her step.

To Do, May 23

- Buy Dad's birthday present!!!!! Soon!!!
- Call Samadhi Spa (or have Genna do it?).
- Remember paper cups tomorrow. And coupons. And aprons.
- Find out what's due in math.

Zoe's Power Up Tea Smoothie!

INGREDIENTS

1 cup black tea, brewed extra
   strong (use 2 tea bags)
1 cup strawberries, fresh or frozen
1 banana
1½ cups plain nonfat yogurt
1 tablespoon ground flax seed
2 tablespoons sugar

Place strong tea in a blender with all
   other ingredients.
Blend until smooth and chug before
   an important match!
Serves 3 players.

Chapter Sixteen

Where there's tea there's hope.
—ARTHUR W. PINERO

The next day at school, I handed Genna and Zoe their Steeping Leaf aprons. Genna was dressed in a tiny skirt with boots.

"Gen, are you a Teashop Girl or a cheerleader?" Zoe asked. "When are we doing this anyway? Lunch?" Zoe was looking calm and well rested for a change.

"Okay, girls, here are the cups and the tea." I was almost drowned out by the eighth-grade basketball captain whistling at Genna's footwear.

"We need hot water," Zoe said, ever practical. Right. Hot water. It occurred to me we hadn't really planned this out.

"No problem. I'll sneak into the booster club office after first period and take the coffeemaker." Genna was so casual; I couldn't believe it.

"Can't we just *ask* to use it?" I looked at Zoe, who shrugged.

"What fun is that? Oh! I have an idea. We should turn up the A/C so everyone is shivery by teatime."

"Turn up the A/C? I'll bet Mr. Arun has the thermostat under his desk." Our principal was famously stingy with the heat *and* air-conditioning. He seemed not to notice the temperature, wearing a green cardigan even when it was over ninety degrees outside.

"Yeah, you're probably right. Well, see you chicas at lunch. Wish me luck with the coffeemaker!" Genna pranced away with a grin before I could seriously protest.

"Why does she *insist* on making the simplest thing a Mission Impossible?"

"Boredom. Did you know Genna's got, like, a beyond-genius IQ?" Zoe said this with complete seriousness as she smoothed her hair into a ponytail using the tie she always kept on her wrist.

"Riiiiiight. Did *she* tell you that?"

"Yeah. You've got a point. Anyway, it feels good to be doing something for the Leaf, you know? That place is our spot." Zoe looked at her yellow apron and I could see her remembering some of our finer moments there. The one good thing about the shop's struggles was that it was reminding Gen and Zo how important the Leaf once was to all three of us. I could see that they really cared. I had the best best friends in the world.

"If this works, it's going to be our spot to share."

"I hope you are right." Zoe hurried off toward homeroom, leaving me at my locker. I pulled out two books and almost created an avalanche—my locker was worse than my bedroom—and checked the stash of tea. I breathed in the peach ginger smell. Soon it would fill a whole wing of the school and maybe a few others would become as obsessed with tea leaves as I am. I crossed my fingers.

Sure enough, Genna plopped an enormous coffeemaker on our corner table three hours later and plugged it in. We started heating water and had tea steeping soon after. The cafeteria took on a peachy smell and people began drifting over to see what was going on. Genna happily poured small cups and added ginormous heaps of sugar, which everyone eagerly grabbed. Anything weird in the middle of a boring school day was big news. And any smell that could mask the lunch lady's Cod Surprise was even better, believe me. Zoe and I handed out coupons and Genna poured until the first batch was out. We quickly got a second batch steeping. Mrs. Peabody, who was on supervision duty that day, wandered over. I poured her an extra-large cup, which she drank with relish.

"Delicious!" she said, and thanked us. We went through three more batches before people stopped coming up. All the coupons had disappeared, and everyone seemed to like the tea except for Zach Anderson, who said it tasted like soapy bathwater. Figures. It backfired on him, though, because Zoe and Genna simultaneously made fun of him for (a) taking baths and (b) drinking bathwater.

"It's just so easy to tease him," Genna said. I couldn't help notice she had winked when he came up to bug us. Gross.

"It's mean to tease lower life forms," said Zoe. "But I think in this case, we're totally allowed."

I couldn't get the grin off my face. The first Steeping Leaf Treat Day had gone so well! I was just about to unplug the coffee machine when Principal Arun appeared. I quickly poured him a cup and offered it to him. He looked angry for some reason.

"What is going on here?" he demanded.

"Treat Day, Mr. Arun. It's tea." Genna smiled her most angelic smile. "Mrs. Peabody said it's delicious."

"Wait! That's the missing coffeemaker from the

booster office! Who gave you permission to use that machine? This isn't a mall food court!" He yelled at us. I was *so* scared. "You three. In my office. Right now. Where is Mrs. Peabody?" The smiles on our faces immediately fell. What was with him? He could get all agitated about the littlest things. We reluctantly headed for the office as Mr. Arun and Mrs. Peabody stayed behind to collect the coffee machine. Zach gloated happily, of course, and scrawled on his notebook, *"The Steeping Reek"* to wave at us. We could hear Mrs. Peabody saying she thought we had permission.

In the office, we all sat in a row, waiting to be admitted to the principal's office. I was freaking out, as was Zoe. I'm sure she was very worried what her parents would say about all this. She was always worried what her parents would say.

I had never once been sent to the office. Which, I realized, was probably a small miracle considering Genna and all her "ideas." Genna wasn't exactly a stranger to the detention hall . . . though she insisted that all her past infractions were *alleged*, not proven. It occurred to me just then that even though I was afraid of what Principal Arun would do, it could be worse. At least he *knew* me and knew that I didn't usually—er, ever—get in trouble. Surely good behavior had to count for something? I was suddenly shivery at the prospect of going off to high school, where now instead of a clean slate I'd have a permanent record. Scary, very scary. I wished that I had saved some of the tea to sip while we waited.

"I can't believe this," Genna was saying. "It's not like we mooned the teachers' lounge, like Zach. Or graffitied the girls' bathroom." She was all flustered. "This is really harsh."

"Look, the important thing is, we stick together," Zoe said with a slightly shaky voice. "Whatever punishment he gives, we all suffer it."

"Zo, that's not fair. I planned it," I said. I patted her hand. No reason for her to smudge her perfect academic record.

"And it was my dumb idea," Genna added. She also reassured Zo, not wanting her to get in trouble.

"I don't care. We stick together. Here he comes." Mr. Arun returned to the office, nodded to the school receptionist, and indicated his office with a frightening tilt of his head. We followed him.

"Who would care to explain?" he asked gruffly.

"I will," I said, with surprising firmness. "We were handing out tea samples because we're trying to save the Steeping Leaf, my grandmother's teashop. It's this wonderful local business over on Monroe Street that's in danger of closing because people insist on going to chain stores, which have no soul, and the building owner is trying to evict us because we're a smidge behind on our rent, and . . ." I trailed off. "Tea is good for people. Better than soda. We were just trying to get everyone to want to go to the shop, give it some business. Show them something different."

"I see. Do you care to add anything?" He looked at Genna and Zoe.

"Sir, it was my idea. We're sorry. We should've gotten your permission," Genna said, her smile making a comeback.

"Yeah. We're sorry." Zoe looked our principal right in the eye. She pushed her white headband back and added, "Did you know that June is National Iced Tea Month?"

"All right. I suppose there was no harm really done. I expect you all to clean up that coffeemaker, put it back where you found it, and next time, *get permission*. I can't have students hawking products like this is some sort of theme park. I'm trying to run a school here."

"Okay, Mr. Arun. Thank you." I let out a breath I hadn't realized I'd been holding. We all smiled at one another and clasped our hands.

"Two more things," he said. *Oh no.*

"First, the next time you decide to bring ginger peach tea to this school, I expect the first mug." There was a sparkle in our principal's eye. "It smelled wonderful." Me and Genna laughed. Zoe handed over the remaining loose tea she had been holding. Mr. Arun nodded in thanks and jotted down the Leaf's address. A new customer, yay! "Two, as for you, young lady," he said, gesturing in Genna's general direction. "I see from your file you've received warnings about this before, so I have no choice but to issue a detention. You can report to room 203 at 3:10."

"If you give her a detention, you have to give all of us one," I said. *Solidarity!*

"Miss Green, this really doesn't concern you."

"If it concerns Genna, it concerns all of us!"

"Very well. If you all want to serve a detention for her skirt, it's fine with me. Good day, ladies." Mr. Arun stood up and we filed out of the office.

American tea drinkers are different from tea drinkers in other parts of the world. Eighty percent of the tea we drink is iced tea. The story goes that it was invented by Richard Blechynden on a hot day in 1904 at the St. Louis World's Fair. No one was visiting the East Indian Pavilion for hot tea until they put their warm drink on ice . . . then they became very popular indeed.

Chapter Seventeen

The first cup moistens my lips and throat. The second
shatters my loneliness. The third causes the wrongs of life to
fade gently from my recollection. The fourth purifies my soul.
The fifth lifts me to the realms of the unwinking gods.

—CHINESE MYSTIC, TANG DYNASTY

Two days later, the *Isthmus* feature story on the Steeping Leaf appeared. It was only a half page, but already business was picking up a bit. Students were even coming in with coupons! I got an A on my "History of Tea" paper, so I'm starting to think I'm a pretty good writer. Of more than just lists, even. That inspired me to write an editorial about supporting local businesses for our student paper. A couple of eighth graders came into the shop to tell me they liked the piece. They only split one pot of tea, but it was a start.

.   .   .

MIDDLE SCHOOL STUDENTS SHOULD SUPPORT LOCAL BUSINESSES
by Annie Green,
barista at the Steeping Leaf Café

Small and locally owned businesses give our town personality. If you want to have the exact same food, clothing, and surroundings as someone in Seattle, a chain is for you. But isn't being young all about finding different ways to express ourselves? How can we do that if we are all drinking the same thing, wearing the same thing, and watching the same thing?

Spending your money in a shop that is owned by someone who lives in Madison means that your money will stay here. Chains are not cheaper or better just because they are trendy. The Steeping Leaf Café, for example, also sells products from local suppliers, which is good for the environment because less gas is used to get foods to the store.

We are sometimes more worried about fitting in than standing out at school, and I think that's sad. It is up to us to decide how we want our world to look, and I for one do not want every single city to be a clone of its neighbor. It might be easier to choose the same brands as your friends, but it's boring.

.   .   .

"I think I have senioritis," Genna declared in a dramatic voice. We were both in the shop after school, willing it to be busier. Genna was flopped over a cushy chair, sipping a warm chai latte and chatting with Louisa, who was being very sympathetic.

Louisa patted Genna's hand and left the counter to me. She went to the patio to see if the few customers outside needed more hot water. I shot Genna an eye roll.

"You are an eighth grader, not a twelfth grader!"

"Fine. Then I have eighth grade—itis. I am so *bored*. My parental units went to Chicago this weekend and just left me again. I think I'll have people over to the pool." She started flipping through her artwork and changing all the $30s to $80s. I know what you're thinking. A pool party in Wisconsin in May? *Brrr*. But Gen's pool is *indoors*. Very posh. I, on the other hand, remember being excited when my dad put a sink and mirror in our basement.

"Gen, don't you think eighty dollars is a little high?"

"What are you saying?"

"Nothing. Anyway, we're going to do a poetry night here next week, and I want you to write something."

"Really? When? Are you going to invite people from school?"

"Monday. I think so." I walked outside to the patio to see if anyone needed anything. Louisa was exchanging pleasantries with the Kopinskis at the biggest table. Ling and Hieu were there too, and sure enough, Louisa held the toddler in her lap. He sat there contentedly, as if he'd been put under a spell. Ling looked at peace too as she balanced her checkbook and sipped a big mug of jasmine tea.

"We loved the *Isthmus* feature," Mr. Kopinski was telling Louisa. "Such a nice story. I didn't know you and Charles opened so long ago!"

"It was all my granddaughter's idea," Louisa said proudly. "Annie called the reporter. Such moxie . . . she reminds me of Charles. I can hardly believe it's been so long myself."

"She really enjoyed interviewing you," I replied shyly, happy to be compared to my grandfather. In fact, Louisa and the lady from the *Isthmus* talked for what seemed like hours. By the end, I was pretty sure we had a new regular customer.

"Oh, Ally was a dear," Louisa said modestly, gently

bouncing Hieu. "Just started getting her own bylines. Such a talented writer."

"I'm glad you both enjoyed the story," I said to the Kopinskis, my voice coming out more confidently as I cleared their plates and wiped up a bit. "I'd really like to see them do another one about the shop . . . we have an anniversary coming up, you know. I'm also thinking of calling *Madison* magazine," I added.

"I admire your chutzpah, Annie," Mr. Kopinski said with a twinkle in his eye. "It seems your grandmother has trained quite the hostess . . . and businesswoman."

"I . . . it's nothing. I just . . . I just really like working here," I said, shy again. *Businesswoman?* Hostess? It sounded so grown-up. "But thank you."

I watered the flowers and checked on the other occupied table. It was Mr. Silverman with one of his huge books. Today, he was intent on one called *The Razor's Edge*. I chatted with him about the weather for a little while and returned to my spot behind the counter to look at Genna. She was sketching on a large white pad. It was a line drawing of the shop itself, and it was beautiful. She had made the room seem bigger and more angular, while perfectly capturing the light on the tables.

"Genna, that is *so* awesome. You should put more sketches like *that* up for sale."

"Whatever, this is just practice. It won't be done until

I splatter it with paint, cut it into strips, and weave it back together."

"Um, okay. Where's Zo?"

"Practice, where else?"

"Check out the fliers I had printed up." I handed over a fat stack of bright orange fliers advertising the shop and its upcoming events.

"Ooh, cool. I like how you put that the Leaf features local artists."

"Thanks."

"When are you going to put these up?"

"Today. As soon as Jonathan gets here to help me."

"Ooh. Operation Save the Leaf Phase Four. Give me some, I can hang them up on my way. Pool party tonight for sure!"

"I thought you were just going to have a few friends over. Gen, won't your parents be upset?"

"Yeah, twenty to thirty of my very closest friends," Genna replied with a wicked smile. "Hey, I'm an only child left home alone with the housekeeper on the weekend. My parents should, like, *expect* me to throw a party. Besides, they are so, like, guilt-ridden over jetting off without me."

"Uh-huh. See you later."

I made sure our staple gun was full and tried to be patient. Finally, Jonathan showed up. He smiled at me and Louisa, who had brought Hieu inside to fetch a cookie.

"What's up, Louisa? I got your message."

"Thank you for coming in, dear. I could use some extra hands today. Help Annie with these fliers, okay?" Louisa handed him a stack and gathered up Hieu, who already had cookie all over his face.

"No prob." He read it over and said, "Just as long as I don't have to write any poetry."

"You never know, Mr. Schultz, you never know. It'd do you some good," Louisa replied.

"I hope this isn't interrupting anything," I said to him as I took off my yellow apron and we headed out to the street. Mmmm. He smelled so good. And I'd managed a complete sentence. This was progress.

"Nah, I'd much rather put up fliers than study. Louisa showed me all your ideas for the store. They're good. I think she's excited about it. I heard her talking about everything with Mr. Silverman."

"Um, cool."

"You know, I think I might have even learned something that I can use for my project."

"Really?"

"Yeah. Like, sometimes a business has to get back to its core values to succeed. I think you're on the right track, I just hope there's enough time . . ."

"Me too," I said emphatically. "Me too." We walked in

silence for a while, and I felt really happy about Jonathan's comment. I prayed I'd think of something clever to say. "So, how's school going? You haven't been here at the shop much." Boring, but it was a start.

"It's okay. How's yours? Do your teachers go all catatonic in front of the overhead projectors like mine did?"

"Yeah. I don't think my social studies teacher has moved a muscle since 1999. They just roll his chair over when they have to mop." I stopped and stapled a few fliers at a kiosk. Jonathan laughed. *We're having a conversation. A real, actual conversation!*

"Sometimes I miss middle school. High school is definitely harder."

"But I'm sure it can be fun." I wished he'd forget I was in middle school.

"Sometimes, yeah. But it's hard being new. That's why I come into the shop to do homework." I had never considered the possibility that Jonathan could be lonely. It seemed the Steeping Leaf was a refuge for more than just me.

"That makes sense."

"Mmm-hmm." Jonathan was silent for a while, stapling fliers methodically to every phone pole we saw. Leave it to me to bring a promising conversation to a screeching halt. I decided to bring up Genna's party. It was a risk. If I decided to go, a swimsuit would be involved.

"So, there's this pool party tonight . . . would you,

um, want to come?" It was one of the scariest questions I had ever asked in my life. I waited, willing myself not to take back the invitation.

"Who's having it?" He stapled loudly and stuck some fliers in people's mailboxes.

"Um, Genna. My friend who's always wearing, um, a beret or something." Genna usually stood out in a crowd because she either had on a blue cowboy hat or a beret. My riskiest fashion choice so far in life was the decision to buy a pair of plaid capris. I never wore them.

"Genna, right. I remember her. Do you think your sister will come?"

"Um, maybe." There was no way Beth would come to an eighth grader's party complete with a chaperone. I immediately felt guilty for suggesting otherwise.

"Cool. What time?"

"Seven? Over on Grant?" I had no idea why my voice was squeaking so much, I was just happy to get the words out at all. I don't remember anything else about stapling fliers after that. I floated back to the shop when a large number of them had been spackled about town and flew home to my computer. Sometimes I wondered if it was more fun to have something actually *happen* to me with a boy or to race home to tell the Teashop Girls about it. It was close. I pushed the thought of Beth and my little untruth out of my head.

Another awesome illustration by Genna. This is the main sitting area in the Steeping Leaf, with all the comfy old-fashioned furniture. Doesn't it make you want to settle in for hours with a nice cup and a good book? I'm surprised people ever go home!

Chapter Eighteen

Find yourself a cup of tea; the teapot is behind you.
Now tell me about hundreds of things.

—SAKI

Genna's dot was green, like it always was, so I shot her a quick message

cuppaAnnie: HE's coming. To your party.

Gengenski00: work it

cuppaAnnie: I don't know what to wear

Gengenski00: bikini of course

cuppaAnnie: r u insane?!?!?!?!?!?

Gengenski00: i might be i hear voices

cuppaAnnie: k good luck with that

I IMed Zoe next. She was almost never available online

to chat, so it was nice to see her tennis shoe screen name pop up.

> **cuppaAnnie:** Jonathan is coming to gen's party
> **Kswiss211:** *who?*
> **cuppaAnnie:** very funny. bring some high school people!
> **Kswiss211:** *what high school people? we're in 8th grade*
> **cuppaAnnie:** i don't know
> **Kswiss211:** *i'm tired*
> **cuppaAnnie:** take a nap, or meditate
> **Kswiss211:** *i am*
> **cuppaAnnie:** i don't think you can at the same time as iming
> **Kswiss211:** *good point*
> **cuppaAnnie:** cu later

After that, I spent two hours trying on clothes, painting my toenails, and carefully examining my face. It was clear for a change, but my freckles were still pretty fierce. Finally, I put on a short pleated skirt and a top over a tankini. Perfect! Well, as close as I could get. My hair went into a ponytail thing that kept it under control. Lip gloss! Where was my lip gloss? I ran into Beth's room.

"Did you take my lip gloss?" I asked. "You know, the expensive stuff?"

"No." She was listening to her French lesson on her iPod at max volume and didn't bother to turn it down. "Why are you so dressed up? We're just going to some Italian place. You know how Dad is addicted to Alfredo sauce and breadsticks. Ugh. Heart attack–ville. I'm getting a salad and that is *it*. Not that I can eat pasta even if I wanted to."

"What?!"

"For Dad's *birthday*. Hello. It's practically all he's talked about for a week."

"Aughhhhh! I forgot about that."

"Just because you're too busy chasing around teashop boy."

"I do not chase teashop b—I mean Jonathan, anywhere. How do you know about that? I can't believe I forgot to get a present."

"If you give me ten bucks, I'll put your name on mine. Cough up." Beth looked at me happily. She always needed money.

"I bet *Mom* gave you the money to buy a present in the first place, but fine. What did you get?"

"A bird feeder, what else?"

"Great. Why haven't we left yet, then? It's almost six."

I couldn't believe that the one time I had actual, nonlame plans, my dad had to go and have a birthday and decide to have dinner so late. I thought about trying to get out of it, but there was no way. My parents think Family Time is, like, holy.

"What's with you? In a hurry to get back here and watch a DVD?" Beth teased.

"No. I'm—none of your business."

Mom called up to us that it was time to go. I grabbed the phone and quickly dialed Genna and Zoe, who promised they would try to keep Jonathan at the party if he actually did show up. It's not that I didn't enjoy spending time with my fam—Billy and Luke could be pretty funny when they decided to stop trying to shoot juice out of their noses—it was just that Jonathan and I had actually talked today. And now he was coming to the party. This night had the potential to be a serious turning point. And I would be spending it eating ravioli and breadsticks.

We picked up Louisa at her little bungalow near the university and all piled into my dad's van. Beth had earbuds in; the boys were fighting. Louisa chatted with my mom about the lovely weather. She was holding a nicely wrapped gift for her son-in-law, never the type to forget to get something, unlike yours truly.

When we arrived, I put my arm around my dad.

"So how does it feel to be eighty-six?" I asked him. He was sporting a special T-shirt for the occasion, which said "Our Business is Monkey, and Business is Good." My dad and his shirts. What were we going to do with him?

Annie's Dad's Favorite T-Shirts
with commentary by Annie Green

"When did my wild oats turn into shredded wheat?" (Okay, who really wants to think about my dad having wild oats? Ew. Also, everyone knows he is old, so is it really necessary to advertise that fact on a T-shirt? Why can't he wear a nice button-down and normal shoes like Zoe's stepdad?)

"I'm your father, not an ATM." (Ha-ha. So funny. Can I help it if a mixed green salad at Tutto Pasta is seven bucks?)

"What if the hokey pokey is really what it's all about?" (What what's all about? I don't get it. Also, if I ever had to see my dad do the hokey pokey, I would die. Another reason for me never to get married or have a wedding reception.)

"The sports team from my area is superior to the sports team from your area." (Duh. Go Badgers!)

"I appreciate the Muppets on a much deeper level

than you." (Um, okay, Dad. If that makes you sleep better at night, good for you.)

"I'll have you know I'm not a day over forty-three." It was true; my parents had been high school sweethearts. *Gag.* He loved to tell the story of how he had stared at Mom's red hair in chemistry—*'nother gag*—and known she was the one. They went to different colleges in entirely different states, but my mom came home for grad school and the rest is Green family history. I guess before they got married, they wrote, like, a million letters back and forth from the East Coast to the Midwest. Can you imagine living before IM? Me neither.

"Happy birthday, Dad."

"Thanks. Now let's see if we can't set a new breadstick record!" What was it with Dad and carbo-loading? I wondered. My dad ran *one* marathon *one* time about a million years ago and still acted like he was in training. But the only part of the training he really did was the carb part. Not so much with the running-every-day part. Well, unless you count chasing my brothers, which I suppose I do.

Thank goodness, we got a table right away. The server came after a century. I kept repeating *hurry, hurry, hurry* in my head and tapping my foot. It took about three years for the drinks to come. Louisa was watching me carefully. Sometimes it wasn't the greatest thing in the universe to have an adult around who was so in tune with your energy, if you know what I'm saying. She just smiled at me and didn't say anything. I smiled back.

Aughh! I gnawed impatiently on my complimentary breadstick. By the time the birthday cake came, it was going to be after eight thirty. Wasn't anyone thinking about the fact that it could get past Billy's bedtime? Was I the only responsible person in the whole family all of the sudden?

"Mom, can we order?" I begged. I shot Beth a look. Once in a while, if Beth was in a really good mood, she'd take my side.

"Yeah, I have a date," she said. *Yes.*

"I'm hungry," Luke whined. No matter that he had had a full meal probably not three hours before. I sent my brother silent telepathic thanks. Everyone finally, finally ordered their dinners. When the meals arrived, I finished mine in three bites, hardly tasting anything. I didn't want my stomach to stick out in my suit. Which I was still wearing. I noticed my mother looking at me curiously. That was the thing about moms, even my own. They could tell in three nanoseconds if something was different with you . . . when they were supposed to be thinking about important stuff like chord progressions or whatever.

About seven years later, everyone else finished eating. I ran to the bathroom and called Genna on Beth's phone. I can't believe she let me use it, but like I said, my sister is very occasionally decent.

"Tell me what's going on. I'll be there in a half hour."

"Relax. Jonathan just got here. But he looks pretty uncomfortable."

"Hmm. Is everything under control?"

"What do you mean? Everything's fine, we're just swimming and stuff." *And stuff.*

"All right, I have to go."

"'Kay."

"Bye." I washed my hands and returned to the table, where a bunch of waiters were singing "Happy Birthday" to my dad. He had to be the only person on the face of the planet that was happy to have chain restaurant waiters sing to him. We all passed our gifts over and Dad oohed and ahhed about the birdhouse, a Weedwacker from the boys, some socks made from organic fibers from Louisa, and a first edition Hemingway from my mom. I remembered that for *my* last birthday, I had gotten a new computer and felt guilty about slacking on the gift. I promised myself I'd get Dad something really nice for Christmas. Then I remembered Louisa always talking about how stuff doesn't matter. Hmm . . .

We all piled back into the van once again, returned Louisa to her place with hugs all around, and went home. It was getting late. I didn't think my mom would let me leave even though it was a weekend night. I decided to go the begging route and give about six different phone numbers for Genna's housekeeper and parents. Fortunately, it worked. I had to promise to be home by ten thirty, though, which was *so* harsh. Thank goodness Genna lived close by.

Annie's Tea Pops

INGREDIENTS

2 cups (approximately one small pot) herbal tea, brewed double strength

1 cup orange juice
2 tablespoons sugar

Brew hot tea using double the amount of leaves you usually would. Let steep for 4 minutes, then allow time to cool.

Stir the orange juice and sugar into the cooled tea, then pour the mixture into ice pop molds or ice cube trays, leaving some room at the top.

Place in freezer and wait 3 hours or until solid. Then, take out pops and lick two or three between cannonballs in Genna's pool!

Chapter Nineteen

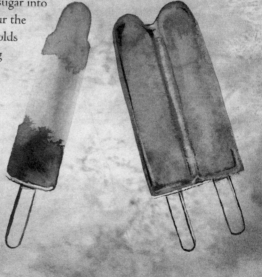

Love and scandal are the best sweeteners of tea.
—HENRY FIELDING, *LOVE IN SEVERAL MASQUES*

I made it to Genna's a bit out of breath. Sure enough, there were a very large number of "close friends" all over the place. I found Zoe, who was wearing a plain Speedo and sitting with her feet in the water, trying to decide if she wanted to get her hair wet. It took forever to dry.

"Hey, how's it been so far?" I asked her, trying not to be too obvious as I craned my neck around, looking for Jonathan. She rolled her eyes.

"He's over there." Zoe pointed, unimpressed. Jonathan was stuffing his face with Genna's Doritos and gulping some sort of energy drink with a lightning bolt on the side. "Annie . . ." She trailed off, and I gave her an *I've-got-this-under-control* smile. Which was funny, seeing as I pretty much never had anything under control.

"I'm going to go find a soda." I wandered off into the main part of the house, only to see Genna and one of her friends from drama club in the den playing DDR . . . in their wet swimsuits.

"Hey, Gen," I yelled over the music, poking my head in the room.

"Annie! You're here!" She abruptly stepped off her dance pad and hugged me. Her skin was cool and her hair was soaked.

"Yes, finally. You're all wet!" I said, a little bit horrified for the carpet. If my mom were here, she'd be in a tizzy.

"Oh yeah, whatever. Anyway, get back out by the pool and your boy! Or wait, see if he wants a tour of the house." Genna grinned, wiggling her eyebrows.

"Um, I'll think about it." I left Gen to her dancing and found the fridge. After I grabbed a soda, I returned to the pool, trying to figure out if I could trust my swimsuit in the water. I wandered over to my target.

"Hi, Jonathan. I'm glad you came." Though I sounded ultra casual and alluring, he just nodded, raised his plastic cup, and jumped into the pool, yelling,

"CANNONBALL!" When he got out and toweled off, I followed him more or less inconspicuously.

"So, where's Beth?" he asked, a hopeful expression on his face.

"Um, actually she couldn't make it. Homework or something," I lied. He looked really disappointed.

"Oh. Well . . . I should probably get going." He toweled off his head and started gathering up his stuff.

I wished that there were some magic words I could say to make him stay and talk to me. Before I could ask Genna what to do, he began talking into his cell phone and putting on his shoes. *I will not cry, I will not cry,* I told myself over and over, quickly wiping my nose. I took a deep breath and tried to forget about Jonathan and his stupid crush on my stupid, stupid sister. Genna came back to the pool and saw Jonathan leave. She looked at me sympathetically and threw her arm around me. When I spoke, my voice actually sounded pretty normal.

"Genna, this place is a disaster." It was. The entire pool room was covered in wet towels, pieces of cookie, flip-flops, and hair bands. Since people had been splashing for over two hours, the pool level was down about a foot and every piece of furniture was soaking wet. Genna didn't care, though. Her face was flushed and there was a flower in her hair (a miracle, given the approximately eleven times she had been thrown in the pool by various boys).

"I know, isn't it great? There must be at least twenty people here!" She sashayed away, saying something about needing more chips, very pleased with herself.

Horror of horrors, who should sidle up just then but Zach Anderson. How on earth had *he* been invited? I took a *laaarge* step away from him and made a face.

"Little Annie Green, teashop girl, at a *party*? Did your mommy say you could?"

"Shut up, Zach. Were you even invited?"

"Oh I *got* invited, Green. Gen-gen is all over my business."

"She is so not, Zach. Ick." I shuddered. Fortunately, some squealing girls at the deep end distracted him and I walked away, feeling like something vile had been spilled on me.

I was just considering jumping into the pool to join a game of chicken (my plan was to pretend my opponent was Beth) when Genna's landline rang. *Uh-oh.* It was after ten thirty. Oops. About three seconds later, Gen's housekeeper appeared and called for me. Embarrassing. Everyone's head swiveled, wondering why I didn't have a cell phone yet. I went to take the call.

"Hello?"

"Annie? Why are you still out? I thought I said ten thirty." My mother's voice sounded impatient.

"Oh. I'm sorry, Mom. I lost track." Why did parents have to be so literal?

"I'd like you to come home. Now."

I tracked down Zoe and explained that I had to leave. She did too, which made me feel a little better. We found Genna, surrounded by a group of freshmen. I suddenly felt angry. It was so unfair that Genna could do whatever she wanted and dress like a twenty-five-year-old fashion designer, while I, Annie Green, had to get home by ten thirty and *work* for spending money. I did some calming breaths like Louisa taught me and pulled Genna away for a second.

"I have to go."

"Aww, already?"

"Yes, Genna." I hugged her with a sigh, told her to throw everyone out soon so her long-suffering house-keeper could go to sleep, and then gathered my stuff. She waved. It was a wasted night. No romance at all, and I hadn't even gone swimming.

Tea Combat

A Zen story
as told by Annie Green

A long time ago in ancient Japan a master of the tea ceremony once accidentally upset a soldier. Even though the tea master said he was sorry, the soldier said they must settle things in a sword duel. The soldier was probably a lot like Zach, from the sounds of things. Anyway, the tea master had no experience with swords, so he asked his friend the Zen master what to do.

When the Zen master was served his tea, he saw how the tea master performed his art precisely, with total concentration and calm. The Zen master said, "Tomorrow, when you prepare to duel, face the soldier and hold your weapon with the same concentration and tranquility with which you perform the tea ceremony."

The next day the tea master did as he was told. The soldier, as he got ready to duel, looked at the tea master for a long time, seeing his fully attentive and calm face. At last, the soldier lowered his sword, apologized for his arrogance, and left.

Chapter Twenty

Tea drinkers are never bored.

—LOUISA

The next day at the Leaf, I was actually busy. It wasn't because we were supercrowded or anything (bah!), but Louisa wasn't feeling well, so I told her to take it easy in the back, promising to bother her only if I was really confused about something. Gift certificates, for example, were still a little terrifying.

Anyway, it was up to me to run the shop, so I didn't really have time to think much about Save the Leaf operations or Jonathan or my homework assignments. It was kind of nice. Instead, I made Ling's cucumber sandwiches, Mr. Silverman's oolong, and several other drinks and snacks. As I was running around and asking after everyone's day, it occurred to me that Mr. Kopinski had been right. I really was a hostess and a businesswoman. Maybe I could handle high school in the fall after all.

At that, the front door chimed and Meg came in with Denise, laden with guidebooks like last time. Their trip must be getting really close. They pulled out chairs from one of our bigger tables and began spreading out. I went over to them.

"Hi, guys," I said, remembering how Louisa had said it was okay to greet younger customers informally as long as I remembered to be more respectful with our older visitors. "You must be taking off soon."

"Hey, Annie." Denise nodded. "Our flight leaves next week. I'm so excited!"

"Yeah, I'm just about packed and everything," agreed Meg.

"Can I get you something to drink?" I asked.

"We'll split a pot of Peach Paradise," answered Denise. I went to prepare the tea and returned to the two friends, eager to hear more about their plans.

"So, where will you visit first?" I looked over all the books closely, yet kept my ears open to what was going on in the rest of the shop in case anyone else needed me.

"We land in Thailand, Bangkok to be exact. We'll spend several days there, then eventually make our way to

Angkor Wat. Our schedule is pretty loose, actually," Meg said, sounding like one of my little brothers at Christmas, all bubbly and animated. She showed me a picture of the ancient temple, which looked like it was straight out of *Indiana Jones*. So cool.

"What an adventure." I smiled. "Maybe someday *I* will do that."

"Maybe someday you will," agreed Meg. "Especially with Louisa's blood in your veins. Is she here?"

"Yes, but she's napping in back," I announced solemnly. "I think it's just a bit of a cold, but I said I could handle things so she could rest."

"Well, it looks like everything is fine," Denise said nicely. "The tea is delicious as usual."

"Thank you."

I checked on the patio and returned to the counter to do a few dishes and straighten our shelves. I adjusted the music volume a bit and made sure we had enough napkins fanned out on the tables. The door jingled and Zach Anderson walked in. I groaned. Not again.

"Hey, Green."

"Zach. What a terrible surprise." He was wearing a shirt and tie, which was very weird. He usually wore expensive, slouchy jeans with a track jacket. "You're looking suspiciously respectable."

"Well, I haven't changed my socks in three days."

"Ewww!"

"So this is where the magic happens. I'll take an iced, tall, double, no-whip, skim, half-caf latte with a shot of vanilla." He tapped his foot. I just stared at him. "Ha-ha, just kidding. I'm going to brunch in a minute. Can I have some water?" I filled a glass and looked at him with my eyebrows raised. As much as the Leaf needed new customers, I didn't really want Zach to be one of them.

"What's up, Zach?"

"I saw your poetry reading signs. I thought maybe I'd stop by and see if this would be a good property for my dad to knock over."

"Very funny." I remembered Mr. Anderson's visit and shivered.

"And you'll be happy to know that the TP has dissolved from my lawn."

"Too bad."

"So Genna's party was interesting." He made a clucking sound with his tongue. "Did you get in *trouble* for being out past ten?"

"It was fun. Such a pity you were there." I narrowed my eyes at him and ignored his question. *What was his problem?*

"Oh, I get around. I even personally watered her lawn on the way home."

"Very mature."

"Thanks. Anyway, you might want to ask your friend what she said about this summer. After you left. Sounds like there will be one less Teashop Girl around."

"Zach, as usual I have no idea what you're babbling about, and I have work to do."

"Fine, I'll see you at school."

"Unfortunately." I glared at him as he wandered out the door with a wave. What was he talking about?

Annie's To-Die-For Cucumber Sandwiches

INGREDIENTS

1 small cucumber, thinly sliced
1 tablespoon lemon juice
½ teaspoon sea salt
¼ teaspoon pepper
1 teaspoon fresh garlic, finely minced

10 slices brown bread, lightly toasted
¼ cup unsalted butter
⅓ cup sour cream

Combine cucumber slices, lemon juice, salt, pepper, and garlic in a bowl.

Butter each toasted side of the brown bread and arrange the cucumber mixture on top of each in layers.

Cut sandwiches in half.

Add a small dollop of sour cream on top and garnish with a thin cucumber sliver.

Serves 5 (unless Zach is around, then serves 2).

Chapter Twenty-One

Meanwhile, let us have a sip of tea. . . .
Let us dream of evanescence, and linger in the beautiful
foolishness of things.

—OKAKURA KAKUZO, *THE BOOK OF TEA*

Genna, what is *with* you today? I *said* Orlando Bloom or Jason Sinowski?" Me and Zoe were chilling out in Genna's pool. We were playing one of our favorite games—Who Would You Rather Be Stranded on a Desert Island With?—before Gen and I had to go back to the Steeping Leaf for its first Official Event. Zoe had refused to write, or listen to, any poetry. She said she'd go to Louisa's herbal remedy workshop, though. Her elbow was always a problem.

"Um, Orlando Bloom. I don't care which football player you offer me, Annie. I'm always going to go with the movie star. Hel-*lo*. How would Jason *Sinowski* help me get discovered once we were rescued?" Genna was subdued; I figured it was probably because her parents weren't too happy about the pool party reports and were being *much* more attentive.

"It's not about what happens when you get rescued," Zoe pointed out. She was floating on an air mattress.

"Okay. Andy Roddick or Jonathan Schultz?" I asked Zoe. Zoe would play the game only if an athlete was included as one of her choices.

"Right. I'm really going to choose Barista Boy and have you start gnawing on my arm. Roddick." Zoe splashed me and Genna floated away.

"Tom Brady or Justin Timberlake?"

"Tom Brady."

"Gen, you look like you swallowed a bug. Come on, your turn," Zoe urged. Genna paddled back to us and tried to come up with something.

"Annie. Sam Jones or Greg Gonzales?" Genna named two cute guys in our class.

"Eh, either. I don't care." I was only interested in sharing my island with one particular boy. I sat on two water noodles and shivered.

"You have to choose!" Genna said loudly. "I mean, there are other guys in the world besides Jonathan." She added, more quietly, "Look, Annie, before you got to my party, Jonathan and I talked a little."

"Really?" I splashed her and my ears perked up. "What did you talk about?"

"Not much."

"Genna, *what* did you *talk* about?"

"Well . . ." She paused for a long time, as if trying to decide how to tell me something bad. "I hate to be the one who has to say this, but your boy is in love with your sister." I saw Zoe and Genna exchange a look, and I sighed a loud sigh. It wasn't anything I didn't know. I just felt really embarrassed that my friends had to tell me. When *they* got crushes on boys, the boys usually crushed right back. It was so humiliating! Why did my mom have to make Beth help that day at the Leaf? Why, why, why?

"I know," I said in a tiny voice.

"Maybe once we're in high school . . ." Zoe offered feebly. I sent her a thankful look but still frowned.

"I'm sorry, Annie. He's not *that* cute," Genna said. She floated over to me and took my hand sort of awkwardly. "I'll help you find another guy, but I don't think it's going to happen this summer." Again, she exchanged a glance with Zoe, and I started to get really worried. Zach's ominous comment, the one I had pushed right out of my mind the moment he said it, reappeared in my head. *Why would there be one less Teashop Girl?*

"What's up, Gen?" I asked, meeting her eyes.

"Well, I'm going away for a little while. I got accepted into this theater camp in upstate New York that starts right after school and lasts for the summer."

"What?" I said. "The whole summer?"

"Yeah," said Genna, "the director in Spring Green recommended me, and it's a pretty big deal. I need to spend these last few weeks of school working with my acting coach to prepare. I can't help anymore with Operation Save the Leaf. I just found out yesterday."

"Oh." At first, what Genna said didn't seem like that big of a problem. I mean, after all, people went to camp all the time. *I* had even gone to camp last year, and it was really fun. Normal camp, that is, not theater camp. But then what Genna said sunk in a little. Just when the Leaf needed her most—needed the Teashop Girls the most— when we were making real progress, she was abandoning it and abandoning me. Why did Genna need to go away to some stupid camp that would turn her into an icky, skinny actress who only went to awards shows and stupid fancy restaurants with one-word names? Was she too good for us now? Why wasn't Madison enough for her? I suddenly felt really angry. Everyone seemed to have forgotten the Leaf, and Jonathan liked Beth and not me. And now my best friend was leaving me when I needed her most. I felt so helpless, and at that moment, the person right before me was Genna and her stupid New York theater camp. All these weeks of working and trying and failing and trying again and stressing about Louisa and the teashop and everything and everyone. I was ready to explode.

"Well that's . . . really dumb."

This ad is funny because it is all about trying to get men to drink tea. Which they totally should! Tea helps to prevent some kinds of cancer and heart disease. And it's good for your teeth. And what guy doesn't want nice teeth? Well, probably Zach, but that's another story.

Chapter Twenty-Two

I always fear that creation will expire before teatime.
—SYDNEY SMITH

I bit my lip. The three of us had never really fought before or said anything even the tiniest bit mean to each other. After all, it was against Handbook rules. But the words hung in the air, and I wished that I could grab them down. Zoe looked back and forth between us. My face flushed red. Genna got up and ran upstairs.

"Annie . . ." Zoe awkwardly put her arm around me. I could tell she didn't know what to say. I squeezed my eyes shut.

"How could she leave, when we promised to save the shop?"

"It's a really good opportunity for her. That place is, like, famous."

"So?"

Zoe was silent for a long time. "Hey—it's not about you." I frowned at her.

"But how could she go behind my back like that and even apply to this place? She's my best friend!" Genna and I talk about *every* tiny detail of our existences. Once we chattered for *four hours* about how to decorate our locker doors (we made magnets with my mom's glue gun; it was totally awesome). It was impossible that something as huge as this could've gone completely undiscussed. I didn't understand how Gen could just decide something without me. I'd never even heard of her "famous" camp.

"Let's talk to her, find out the details. It's not the end of the world, Annie. I'm still here." I blinked back tears and sniffled, following Zo out of the pool. "Genna? Come out. Where are you?" Zoe called.

"I'm in my room." A small voice came from upstairs.

"Come down."

After an eternity, Genna came out. She looked annoyed and glared at me. "It would be nice if my *best friend* could be happy for me."

"How long are you gone for?" I glared back, crossing my arms. I'm not proud of it, but it's what I did.

"Look, aren't you even going to apologize and congratulate me?" Genna pouted a bit. Her dramatic side wasn't making the situation any better. I could feel my cheeks flush red in anger.

"We need you here."

"No, you don't. Not really. I mean, come on. How much can we do anyway? We're in *eighth grade*. If the Leaf closes, it closes. Tough cookies, life goes on." Genna crossed her arms. *So there.*

"I can't believe you. I thought you had faith in us. Was all of that work a joke to you? Does the teashop even *matter* to you?" I could feel this terrible weight on my chest. Genna didn't think we could actually make a difference. Perhaps she *never* thought we could, and was only humoring me and my little-girl world.

My eyes filled with tears. Maybe helping out at the Leaf was just a phase for Gen. She didn't really care about it after all. I couldn't hold back my anger. All my frustration came pouring out in one rambling sentence.

"You get whatever you want, Genna, and when you're bored with something you are done with it . . . now you're bored with helping with the Leaf and you're probably bored with me and now your dumb theater camp is more important to you than the place where we spent our childhood and it's more important than our friendship."

"Get a grip, Annie. It's just a stupid teashop. We're too old for it anyway." Genna shot back. It was as if she was talking to me from very far away.

"How can you even say that?" I felt like I might explode.

"How can you call my camp dumb?" Genna replied, her eyes flashing.

"All right, we're leaving." Zoe could see that I was too angry to be reasonable, so she dragged me out of there. I glared at both of my friends but left with Zo, mostly because she had my wrist.

"So much for the Teashop Girls," I muttered as we collected our bicycles and started to ride home.

"Annie."

"If it's not about her, she doesn't care about it. She's unbelievable. You can't be too old for tea." I was shaking.

When we arrived at my doorstep, she hugged me and said, "It's going to be okay. Go take a nap for a little while and try to calm down. I can still help, and Gen didn't mean it. She *does* care about your shop." I noticed Zoe said "your shop," not "our shop." I frowned at her.

"You sound like my grandmother." You know what the thing is about people who are all reasonable and Zen? They can be really annoying.

I ran up to my room, shut the door, put on some music, and pulled out my homework. Since I was probably going to die without ever kissing a boy or saving the Leaf, I might as well get straight A's.

Louisa has a silver tea service a lot like this one. It was given
to my great-great-grandmother Sarah on her wedding day.
Her parents escaped the famine of Ireland and she was the first
child in the family born here in the United States. It makes me
happy to think of so many generations of women using the
same tea service.

Chapter Twenty-Three

There is a great deal of poetry
and fine sentiment in a chest of tea.
—RALPH WALDO EMERSON

The poetry night was pretty much a disaster. I was too distressed to read the Pablo Neruda poem Louisa helped me pick out. I quietly introduced the five people who showed up, including Mr. Silverman. He could tell I wasn't in the mood to talk poetry, and I could see that he was disappointed and a touch confused. Zoe came to make me feel better and read the poem that Genna had written for the event but was *too* busy practicing with her acting coach to come. I tried to figure out its hidden meaning, but it sounded like complete nonsense. Even though I was still in a fog of icky feelings over my fight Genna, I couldn't help but smile a bit at the faces Zoe made while trying to get through the strange verses. Her voice wavered slightly as she read:

"My heart
like gravy or a growing vine
the ocean reef, the new bird's song
Who needs to hear
a word a whisper
forever forever or never never
ask no questions, it will be tomorrow soon."

Zoe was a girl who usually read things like Lance Armstrong's autobiography, not stream-of-consciousness teen babble. She had to practically shake herself off when she was done. Louisa and Zoe chatted for several minutes. My grandmother asked after her parents, her meditating, and her tennis game, and Zoe tried some of the shop's newer tea varieties. We didn't mention Genna, and Louisa, noticing my cloudy face, didn't ask.

Though my grandmother seemed unconcerned at the low turnout and reassured me that it was an enjoyable evening, the quiet night had put me in an even worse mood. After it was over and everyone had shuffled out, I put away the microphone and stared at Louisa's herbal remedy chart.

.   .   .

Astragulus: diuretic, strengthens lungs, enhances immune
 function

Chamomile: soothing nerve tonic, aids insomnia

Echinacea: immune-system stimulant

Feverfew: migraine headache prevention

Garlic: blood pressure regulator, detoxicant

Ginger: digestive aid, fights nausea and stomach ailments

Gingko: increases blood flow to the brain, stimulates all
 blood vessels

Ginseng: energizer, immune-system strengthener

Milk thistle: treats liver disorders by stimulating production
 of new cells

Parsley: diuretic that helps eliminate all kinds of fluid
 retention

Red clover: anti-inflammatory

Rose hips: source of vitamin C, nourishes skin

Sage: stimulates the brain, improves memory

St. John's Wort: treats headaches and mild melancholia

Yerba mate: powerful stimulant, weight-loss aid

.   .   .

It seemed clear that there was a cure for practically everything except a broken heart and a disloyal best friend.

"Would you like some rose hips, dear? Your color is a
bit off." It was just like Louisa not to ask me exactly what

was the matter. I nodded and we sipped her restorative brew quietly. After a long while, I asked her a question.

"Why do the things we care about have to change?" I said this sort of into my teacup, but Louisa heard me. She brushed a strand of my curly hair back behind my shoulder and rearranged her scarves.

"I don't really know the answer to that, sweetie. But I do know that sometimes change can be for the better."

I snorted, wondering how. She smiled kindly.

"Sometimes things we care about move away to make space for other things. Take Beth for example. She's going away to college, which is sad for us. But now you get a bigger bedroom, right? The universe provides. But not always according to orders."

"You can say that again." Louisa *was* right about the bedroom though.

"Well, what if it did? What if we always got exactly what we asked for? There would be no mystery, no surprises."

"That'd be nice," I replied. If I got exactly what I asked for, things would be different, let me tell you. Among other things, I'd have straight, silky hair like Zoe's.

"Maybe. Maybe not. How's your tea?"

"It's good, Louisa. Thanks." I actually smiled a little. That's the thing about my grandmother. You can't stay depressed around her, even when you try.

"There will always be tea, dear." With that, Louisa fetched a piece of carrot cake and two forks. I shared with her, not cured of my mood exactly, but feeling better. She was, of course, right. At least about the tea.

I walked home and threw my work clothes in the wash. My family was all watching a movie in the living room. I joined them wordlessly. Truman found my lap and snuggled in. After the movie, I went to my desk. If Genna was going to just ditch the Teashop Girls, we were going to have to move on without her.

Possible Teashop Girl Replacements

- One of Zoe's teammates?
- Smart girl transfer, what's her name, Katie?
- Stacy, the seventh grader on AIM all the time?

Speaking of which, Stacy was on AIM now. I clicked.

cuppaAnnie: Hi Stacy

Spaciezz91: Annie! Did you hear what Zach did during lunch?

cuppaAnnie: No, and I can't say I want to

Spaciezz91: Oh

Spaciezz91: r u sure?

cuppaAnnie: Yes. So what are you up to this
weekend?

Spaciezz91: prolly beach or mall

Spaciezz91: dunno

cuppaAnnie: so what else is new

Spaciezz91: I'm going out with the new kid, the transfer

cuppaAnnie: you have a boyfriend, too?!

Spaciezz91: well I've always been mature for my age

cuppaAnnie: right

Spaciezz91: don't worry I could find you a bf

Spaciezz91: how about Zach?

Spaciezz91: or that kid with the blond fro

cuppaAnnie: Ewwww. And I don't know the blond
kid

Spaciezz91: I could ask him out for you

cuppaAnnie: NO!

Spaciezz91: k whatev hey I liked your tea

cuppaAnnie: thanks

Spaciezz91: i have this special herbal tea from china that's
sposed to make boys all crazy for you

cuppaAnnie: you believe that?

Spaciezz91: sure, why not

cuppaAnnie: sounds kinda weird

Spaciezz91: well I do have a bf don't i?

. cuppaAnnie: yeah

cuppaAnnie: gotta go

Spaciezz91: bye

Well, that was four minutes I'll never get back, I thought as I shut down the computer. I crossed Stacy off the list. Six times.

To Do, May 31

- Plan Steeping Leaf 30th anniversary party
- Conduct ritual burning of Teashop Girls Rules and Handbook
- Call Zoe
- Convince Mom to change my curfew since 10:30 is way gulag
- Remind reporters about SL anniversary
- Write ANOTHER essay for Mrs. Peabody
- Practice crow yoga pose

Do you know what a tea plant looks like? Well, here you go, a Genna Matthews original sketch of the Camellia sinensis. This is where all the magic starts!

Chapter Twenty-Four

Afternoon tea should be provided, fresh supplies,
with thin bread-and-butter, fancy pastries, cakes etc.;
being brought in as other guests arrive.
—MRS. BEETON, *THE BOOK OF HOUSEHOLD MANAGEMENT*

I had spent most of the night tossing and turning, trying to decide if I should just leave the fate of the teashop to the adults and maybe go back to just visiting like I used to, before getting my job. That way I could at least avoid Jonathan and future humiliation. I knew there would be some peace to be found in a "whatever will be, will be" attitude. But it just wasn't me. I could never be okay with not doing absolutely everything I could think of to save the shop. By the morning, the answer was completely clear. We'd just have to carry on without Genna's help. I really loved the place and my grandmother, and I would never give up. The work we had done so far was leading to good things; it would be silly to quit, no matter what Gen had said.

I got ready for school, washing my face while Beth flat-ironed her hair. We were running a little late, which was typical since Beth had no first-period class and senior privileges. She was never in a rush in the morning. I tried not to make it too obvious that she was not exactly my favorite person. After all, that tiny, truthy part of my brain reminded me that she couldn't help Jonathan's feelings and she would never date a high school sophomore now that she was practically in college. Duh.

After second period, Genna ran up to me. She tried to corner me in the bathroom, but I escaped.

"Forget it, Genna. I don't want to talk about it." It's not that I decided to give her the silent treatment, exactly. She said what she said and I said what I said and as far as I was concerned, there was nothing left to say. At lunch, Zoe sat by me and Genna sat by some of the arty people.

"You should just talk to her, Annie. This is ridiculous. We've been friends forever," Zoe pestered.

"Yeah, and now we can *not* be friends forever. I am burning the Handbook."

"Look, she feels really bad about what she said. She does believe we can save the shop. She doesn't think it's stupid at all."

"She should feel bad," I replied, digging into my chicken salad.

"It was just a meaningless fight, Annie."

"I guess." It wasn't meaningless to me, though. I couldn't really explain why, I just knew that what Genna had said hurt me more than even the Jonathan-and-Beth debacle. Things were changing in all of our lives, as much as I didn't want to admit it; we were growing up and, it seemed, growing apart. I couldn't stand it that there was no more Teashop Girls, not really. I had wished maybe there always would be.

"Yeah . . ." Zoe paused for a little while. I chewed unhappily.

"You heard what she said about the shop. Do you believe in it, Zo? Are you still a Teashop Girl?"

"Annie, I *do* believe in it. And I am. But you should know that even if there is a day when there is no teashop, we'll still be best friends."

I sniffed.

"Think about all the stuff you have that Genna doesn't. Normal parents, for one. Who actually listen to you and care what you do. This theater camp thing is big for her."

"Whatever." I sighed. Zoe was wearing me down. She had always been so *reasonable*, even when we were kids. Well, except on the tennis court.

"Okay, you can mope around for a couple more days and I'll leave you alone about it. But just promise me you aren't going to break up the Teashop Girls for good."

"I'll think about it."

Later that night, I flipped the lights on in my room. There were several e-mails from Genna on the computer, but I didn't open them. After all, I had more important things to think about besides ex-friends. There was a party to plan at the Steeping Leaf (which meant more e-mailing newspapers and putting up fliers and decorating and cajoling classmates and all the neighbors into coming), and Louisa had asked me to do double duty at the shop the next day, looking after the little grandniece of one of her friends near the end of my shift after school. Louisa knew I would make sure little Tameeka would receive the finest education in all things having to do with tea and cookies. I was actually looking forward to it.

I went out for a paddle with my dad in the evening because I was still feeling guilty about forgetting his birthday and I hadn't spent much time with non-Louisa family members in so long. We live near a quiet lake called Wingra that borders a nature preserve owned by the university, called the arboretum. It's a great place to get the canoe out, and we try to do it a few times per year when the weather is nice. This would be our first time this spring. Sometimes we don't even talk that much, we just—what's the word?—*synchronize* our oars and go. Like Louisa, my dad is good at spotting wildlife when we are on the lake. I think he's happy I like to go out, because Beth is really prissy about outdoors activities, and the boys are even spazzier than me, if you can believe that. They are too young to just paddle and "appreciate nature." For a change, my dad was wearing a shirt with no writing on it. I think he didn't want to disturb the wildlife. Or maybe he forgot to finish the laundry.

"Come on, I want to steer this time," I told him, climbing into the back of the canoe. He protested, but I won. I knew I would have to paddle really hard, but it would be fun. I got my feet wet as I pushed us off, but then hopped in like an expert. We were off.

"Mmm, smell that algael air," my dad said happily. He grew up on a lake up north and nothing made him happier than the peculiar smell associated with a good bloom of the green stuff. Ew.

I guess one of the ways we were similar, though, was that it was the simpler things in life that made us smile. A cup of tea for me, a dripping oar for him. I was really glad we decided to go out on the water.

"Where is that one spring?" I said. "I know it's around

here somewhere." I shared a terrible sense of direction with my mom, so even though we'd been to the spring before, I had no idea which way to steer us. Fortunately my dad pointed the way. It *was* beautiful outside. The clear water was a favorite of large birds and long muskie fish. We hugged the edge of the lake, in the shallows thick with vegetation and the lively sounds of insects.

"Turn right. Slowly, slowly. Careful!" my dad said. Sometimes I forgot to use the good techniques he had shown me and got a little wild. I paddled with all my strength, but we weren't really getting anywhere. The trouble was I weighed so much less than my dad, so I really shouldn't have been in the back. I half stood up and almost tipped us over.

"Annie! Wait." My dad was paddling us back to shore so we could make the switch safely. I didn't want to wait, though, so I inched back up again. This time, I slipped a little and ended up sprawled on the bottom of the canoe. I burst into tears.

"Sweetie, don't worry. It's okay. Just stay there." My dad leaned back a little to give me a pat and paddled calmly. "The muskie are all licking their lips."

At that, I laughed a little. I didn't want to be muskie lunch. My dad looked at me quizzically. After already going through Beth's teen years, he was pretty understanding about the mystery-tear routine. But I knew I would have to offer *some*thing in the way of explanation for my sniffling.

"I'm so sick of waiting around all the time while everything is changing all around me," I said with a big sigh.

"Huh? You never sit still for longer than ten minutes."

"That's not what I mean. It's just that Genna's so grown-up and Zoe . . ." I couldn't really think of anything about Zoe to complain about, so I stopped talking. Then I said, "I mean, Genna won't even be around this summer to help with the Leaf! Or care," I added quietly.

My dad sighed. "I wonder if maybe you've taken on too much, honey."

I knew he meant my job (er, crusade), so I quickly protested.

"Don't be in such a rush to grow up, Annie. When you *are* a grown-up, trust me, you'll wish you were a kid again. But maybe not a teenager, I suppose." He paused, smiling a bit. I realized I should ask him sometime about what it was like when *he* was about to start high school. "Anyway, it's not so bad letting your old dad do most of the paddling sometimes, you know. And I promise Louisa will be just fine, no matter what happens. She is one tough cookie, you know."

"I know." It kind of made me smile a little to compare

my grandmother in her flowing scarves to some sort of television-detective-tough-cookie type.

"I'm sorry about the Leaf, honey. I know how much it means to you."

"Yeah, I'm sorry too." We were quiet for a moment. I could see it really bothered my dad that he couldn't fix what was wrong with a Band-Aid and an ice-cream cone like when I was younger. In a strange way, I felt sorry not just for myself at that moment, but also for him. Isn't getting older *weird*?

"Just try not to stand up again. When the fish ask what's on the menu, I don't want to say Annie Surprise."

"*Dad*, really."

This is an ad for tea made with young leaves, which have more caffeine than older leaves . . . so, this Tender Leaf tea made its drinkers very "lively." Today we call tea made from young leaves and buds white tea. Louisa has about six kinds of white tea at the Steeping Leaf. They are very popular. I guess Madison "likes it lively"!

Chapter Twenty-Five

One sip of this will bathe the drooping spirits in delight,
beyond the bliss of dreams.

—JOHN MILTON

At the shop the next afternoon, I went back
and forth between manning the register and
talking about the thirtieth-anniversary party
with Louisa.

"What kind of food would you like to have, dear?" She
flipped through one of her favorite French cookbooks, with
a shopping list at her side. Louisa may do yoga every day,
but trust me, she isn't one of those types who eat mostly
brown rice and vegetables. Julia Child (with her "lots of
butter" philosophy) was her favorite chef, and the scones
and other pastries in the shop were all perfected long ago
by Louisa, working together with a local baker.

"I'm not sure, Louisa. What do you think?" Now that I knew how to make tea and espresso, I figured I should really learn to bake. But I didn't have any ideas.

"Maybe some classics, like the cucumber sandwiches with no crusts—I know you love those, dear—and something completely new. A cake, perhaps. There's a recipe I want to try with toffee that should have the whole neighborhood licking their lips." Usually, Louisa's new recipes made me smile and excitedly start gathering ingredients, but today I just said, "Sure, that sounds okay." My perfect level of cheer was nowhere to be found.

"Are you all right, Annie, love?" Louisa asked in the middle of our planning. She made a note on a shopping list that included things like heavy cream and butter. "You still seem a little blue, dear."

"Nah, I'm fine. Just problems with, you know, friends. Boys."

"I see. Friends and boys do tend to vex the best of 'em." Louisa nodded, watching me.

"They sure do. Stupid vexers. Who needs them?"

"Oh, I don't know. Most people need friends." Louisa smiled.

"Not me," I said.

"I suppose you have your blues to keep you company."

"I guess I do." We worked quietly for a little while, with

Louisa watching me silently. I tried to seem more upbeat.

"Annie, I need to tell you something." She said this very softly.

"What's up, Louisa?"

"I've made a decision." Even more softly. What was this, a library? Why were we whispering?

"A decision about what?" I whispered back.

"About the shop. I'm afraid it affects you, dear."

"Uh-oh." This did not sound good. I stood up straighter and smoothed my apron, ready for business. "I promise I'll be in a better mood. I'm sorry. I'll—"

"Annie, Annie, sweetheart, stop. You've been fine. Better than fine, amazing. Nevertheless, we'll both be done with barista-ing soon."

"Why?!" I wailed. I couldn't believe my grandmother would give up already. Not when things were starting to get better.

"I'm going to close the Steeping Leaf. I've really appreciated all that you and the girls have done . . . the cleaning and the fliers, the Samadhi Spa trip, and now the party planning. I've given this decision days and days of careful thought and meditation, dear. But I'm afraid that instead of an anniversary party, what we're having is a farewell party."

"But, but . . . younger people were coming in . . . the newspaper stories! The Kopinskis are here every day almost. And Mr. Silverman and little Hieu . . ." I started to trail off, then added, "It's only a matter of time before the Leaf is just like it was before."

"The Steeping Leaf will never be just like it was before, Annie. Nothing ever is."

"But . . ."

"I'm sorry, love. I know you're disappointed." Louisa hugged me close, just like she had when I was little. It didn't help this time, though.

I was more than disappointed. I was crushed. I had certainly not won Jonathan's heart; I had broken up the Teashop Girls. And I had failed to save the one thing that mattered to me the most. My beloved Steeping Leaf. I was suddenly very afraid that my grandmother really *would* move away forever. Hadn't she just been talking to Mr. Silverman the other day about how harsh our last winter had been? Oh no!

"I realize this isn't the best spirit with which to plan a party, Annie, but I hope you'll still help. I can't do it alone."

"Of course, Louisa." I sniffled. After a few moments of sitting and thinking about it all, of wishing we had tried this or that, I got up. I noticed a familiar face at the door. It was Mr. Anderson, Zach's dad. He had a pretty blond lady with him, probably Mrs. Anderson. She was petite and wore a demure suit with small jewelry. It was hard to believe she could've spawned Zach and his loud mouth. I asked if they would like something to drink, but they told me they just wanted to have a look around. I had to hold back tears as I watched the Condo King and his queen survey the Leaf. It was hard not to jump in and start babbling about all the nooks and crannies of the shop that made it so irreplaceable. From the bird's nest outside to the height markings on the back door for me and all my siblings, the Leaf was home. All I could do, however, was stare at them unhappily. I remembered Zach's taunt about the bulldozer and wondered how I'd ever be able to sit in the same classroom with him again.

Be the river, be the river. I repeated Louisa's river mantra about flowing peacefully over and around the pebbles of life. *Well, if it has to be this way,* I said to myself, *we may as well throw the best farewell party the town has ever seen.* There were so many details to attend to; I was starting to feel overwhelmed. I was relieved when Jonathan arrived to put up the party fliers. For once it wasn't because I was aching to see him, it was because it was one less thing for me to do. He stopped at the counter and filled up a to-go cup of water.

"So that party at your friend's last week was pretty fun, Annie. Sorry I couldn't stay long."

"Uh, yeah. It was good."

"Where are your friends today? The Teashop Girls? I thought they came here every time you had a shift." He smiled and I frowned. There were no Teashop Girls.

"I don't know." It came out more sharply than I meant it to.

"O-kay . . ." He backed away a little bit.

"Sorry, I'm just a little stressed about things. The Steeping Leaf is closing."

"Yeah, Louisa told me. I know. I'm sorry, Annie." He seemed to try to find something else to say, then gave up. "So, are these all the fliers?"

"Yes." He grabbed the stack and the staple gun and strolled out the door. I watched him go, a pang in my chest. I was starting to understand that no matter what, Jonathan was never going to look at me as anything but an overambitious coworker. He would never care about my thoughts on world peace or my reasons for thinking avocadoes were the world's most perfect food or my well-developed opinions on why tea was better than coffee. I was just a kid who made him put up fliers all the time for a tiny place he probably cared very little about. I sighed.

I called all the newspapers and magazines in the area to get the Steeping Leaf party placed on their calendars. I also made sure to remember to invite all the longtime customers and our neighbors.

"Are you Annie?" A hurried-looking elderly woman rushed through the shop door, five-year-old in tow. "This is Tameeka. Louisa arranged to watch her for a few hours?"

"Yes, hi there. I'm Annie Green. Nice to meet you." I shook hands with Tameeka and made an effort to grin. It wouldn't do to take out my frustrations on a cute little kid. The little girl moved shyly behind her great-aunt's legs.

"Would you like to have some tea and cookies with me? It's almost four o'clock. That's when the Queen has *her* tea and cookies." Tameeka came out of hiding and nodded. Her great-aunt smiled and hurried off, assuring me that the little girl would be picked up by her mother at seven.

"What's that?" Tameeka said, pointing at Genna's Popsicle painting.

"That's bad art," I answered with a serious expression.

"What's that?" she said again, this time looking at a chessboard set up neatly on a coffee table in front of a couch. She carefully picked up one of the pieces, decided she liked it, and grabbed a whole handful of others. I rushed over.

"That's a chess set. Let's leave those here right now." I placed Tameeka on a chair and pushed it close to the table so she would have a hard time getting out. I poured her some lukewarm sweetened tea and arranged a plate of small cookies.

"So, Tameeka, what are you learning in kindergarten?"

"Spelling. And shapes. An oct-o-gon-o-don has eight sides."

"Wow, you must be the smartest kid in your class."

"I am," Tameeka said seriously. "I know how to spell 'Saturn' and I know how to add ten plus two and I know where babies come from!"

"That's impressive." I had no wish to discuss where babies came from with a five-year-old, so I changed the subject. "Have you ever had tea before?"

"Um, um, yes. No." Tameeka spilled a little and ate a cookie in one big bite.

"Do you like it?"

"Yes. But I like the cookies more. How old are you?"

"I'm thirteen . . . well, I'm going to be fourteen soon."

"That's old."

"I know."

"I'm five."

"That's how old I was when I first started coming here with my friends."

"Really? What are their names?" Tameeka asked with crumbs flying.

"Zoe and Genna." I stopped.

"I have two best friends, too. Their names are Jackie

and Kaitlyn, and we do everything together all the time." Tameeka happily jabbered on about all the fun things she liked to do with Jackie and Kaitlyn. I missed being together with my two best friends. I really, really, really missed them. I rarely remembered anything from that far back, but suddenly an image of the three of us filled my mind. We were sitting near the same table Tameeka and I were now, coloring and eating muffins while our moms chatted nearby. Genna had dropped her muffin on the floor and started crying. I had split the rest of mine with her . . . or had it been the other way around? I looked at Tameeka. "My friends had a special club called the Teashop Girls."

"I want to be a Teashop Girl!"

"You do, do you? Okay." I stood up and got a piece of paper and some tape. I carefully cut out the shape of a heart and drew a picture of a teacup on it. I taped it to Tameeka's shirt. "I hereby declare you an honorary member of the Teashop Girls."

"Yay!" Tameeka clapped her hands.

"Yay!" I said in response. And got an idea.

The Steeping Leaf Traditional Chai Iced Tea

INGREDIENTS

1 quart water
½ cup black tea leaves
4 star anise, ground
½ tablespoon powdered vanilla
½ teaspoon clove powder

¼ teaspoon chopped cinnamon
¼ teaspoon ground ginger
½ to 1 cup unrefined cane sugar
Ice cubes
1 pint coconut milk

Bring the water to a boil.

Place the tea, anise, vanilla, clove, cinnamon, and ginger in a big teapot.
Pour the water over the tea and spices and let steep until cool.
Add sugar to taste.

Strain into a clean covered pitcher. Let the tea finish cooling to room
temperature, then refrigerate until ready to serve.

Fill 4 tall glasses with ice cubes and add tea to three quarters full.
Add ½ cup coconut milk to each glass and serve with a straw.

Serves 6

Chapter Twenty-Six

Perhaps you would like some tea as soon as it can be got.

—JANE AUSTEN, *MANSFIELD PARK*

Annie, it's Genna. Call me back." Genna had started leaving a message every day on my family's phone. I was having a tough time explaining to my mom why Genna and I were no longer friends.

"Look, Mom, I think she's a bad influence. I've got other friends!"

"I just don't understand, Annie. She calls here sounding sadder every day. What happened?"

"Nothing, Mom. We're just growing apart."

"Uh-huh. You went from attached by your dangly earrings to growing apart in one week?"

"It happens." I wandered out of the living room, leaving my mom looking confused. Both of my parents were giving me a lot of concerned looks since hearing about the fate of the Leaf. My mom was more worried about me than she was about Louisa. I guess my grandmother knew a lot more about "being the river" than I did. She was serene, whereas I was a ball of upset. Fortunately, I had other things to think about. Making Tameeka an honorary Teashop Girl had been super inspiring. Before the farewell party, I had a hundred pink buttons and stickers made up for all the little girls in the Leaf's neighborhood. We handed them out in the shop during our last week. They loved them. Girls seemed to adore the idea of teatime because it meant pretty dishes, lovely foods, nice drinks, and sharing stories. Even the very little ones seemed to understand right away how fun it could be to stop everything at four o'clock and have a warm drink and a tiny sandwich with the crusts cut off.

Zoe came in to keep me company before the big party. She even put on a skirt (white, of course) for the occasion, which is something Zoe had not done willingly—off the court—in a very long time. I was wearing a new sundress. Beth, who was being very nice since she heard about the Leaf closing, had helped me do my hair. It was very curly and there were a few little flowers in it, above my ears. Louisa had everything set for food; people would be arriving in less than a half hour. Invitations had gone out to dozens of Louisa's friends. Combined with the hundreds of fliers floating through campus and the Vilas neighborhood, it was sure to be an impressive gathering. We had even decided to borrow some extra folding chairs from a restaurant a few blocks over, just in case. Some of Louisa's friends weren't exactly young anymore, even if they did do yoga.

I had to break the news to Zoe that the Steeping Leaf would be closing the following week. I just blurted it out, not really knowing what to say. Zoe couldn't believe it at first. Despite her usual matter-of-fact demeanor, her eyes welled up and she touched all the shelves of tea wistfully. Both of us sat quietly for a few moments, being sad for our special place, the broken up Teashop Girls, and the fact that, like it or not, things didn't stay the same. It was kind of strange to spend so much time with only Zoe. I realized that it had usually been Genna and I, with Zoe joining us when she could. I knew that our fight made Zo very sad, and that made me feel worse about it, torn between my two friends. *Ahem,* I mean friend and ex-friend. After a little while, I scooted my chair closer to Zo, who hugged me fiercely and tried to get herself together. After all, the party that night was to be a celebration of good memories.

"I'm going to miss this place."

"Me too."

"So you know how my stepdad likes his car cleaner than an operating room?" Zoe sniffed and changed the subject as I brewed some fresh iced tea and straightened the huge banner that said WE LOVE YOU, STEEPING LEAF. She was plopped down at the counter, awkwardly pulling on her skirt.

"Yeah?"

"Well, my mom asked me to go with her to pick up some groceries last week, so we took his car as usual. We have to be all careful to wipe our shoes before we get in and stuff and make sure we don't leave any fast food wrappers. So we go grocery shopping, bring the bags in, and that was that."

"So?"

"Well, that would be the end of the story had we not forgotten a *cantaloupe* in there. It rolled out of the grocery bag, I guess, and nestled in a tight spot behind the jumper cables. It had been in there for four days. In the heat, all through the storm and everything. My mom opens the trunk this morning and starts laughing. The cantaloupe had burst open and it was *everywhere*. So we pull the car out of the garage—thank God my stepdad is out on the motorcycle—and get to work picking about a million seeds and rotten melon bits out of the trunk. I'm thinking, 'He'll never have to find out, we'll get this all cleaned up even if it takes two hours.' I'm hanging out of the trunk, butt in the air, when who should come home early but him."

"Oh, no."

"Eh, he was actually really nice about it. But my mom says she gives it three days before he starts shopping for a new car. We couldn't get *all* the seeds. What're these?" Zoe picked up all of my pink Teashop Girl buttons. I giggled at the thought of Zoe hanging out of a trunk trying to Shop-Vac melon seeds. It almost put me in a good mood.

"I've been giving them to the little girls who come in with their parents. They're going nuts for them. Louisa says she wished we would have started this months ago."

"These are Teashop Girl buttons."

"Yeah."

Zoe was silent for a minute.

"What?"

"It's just that it bums me out. You've, like, *franchised* us even though the Teashop Girls are history."

"What are you talking about?"

"Seriously, Annie. *We* were the Teashop Girls. You, me,

and Genna. You can't just let all these other people in after you've kicked a founding member out."

"Zo, they're, like, five. They love it."

"I don't care. You should've gotten our permission."

"Oh." I paused. "I'm really sorry, Zo. I didn't think of it that way."

"Well, you should have."

"I'm sorry."

"Call Genna. Invite her to the party. You can't make every kid in Madison a Teashop Girl if the original Teashop Girls are in shambles. It wouldn't even mean anything then."

"No."

"Annie, don't you remember? It was *Genna's* idea to start the Handbook. And it was Genna's idea to do the sidewalk chalkings and the free samples at school and the spa trip. She's done more for the Leaf than *I* have. By lots! It was just a stupid fight. Neither one of you meant what you said, and you *know* she loves you. Now stop being stubborn and call her."

"No," I said, but my voice was very small. Zo made a pretty good point. Regardless of what Genna planned to do this summer, she *had* done everything she could think of to help the shop. I remembered our gleeful chalkings during Phase One and suddenly felt really bad for how selfish I was being. Still, I was too confused to admit it.

"Call Genna, or I'm leaving, too, and taking your buttons with me. . . ." She narrowed her eyes.

"Okay, okay." I reached for the phone. "She can come to the stupid party. I don't care."

"Good."

I called Genna, whose number, I admit, I will probably remember until I die.

"Hello? It's me. Yeah. Okay. I know. Anyway, are you doing anything tonight? Well, there's a party . . ."

True Friends

A Zen story
as told by Annie Green

Many ages ago in China, there lived two best friends who were very close, just like me and Genna and Zoe. One friend played the harp with great ability, and the other friend listened with great ability.

When one played about a mountain, the other would say, "I can see the mountain!"

And when one played about the stream, the other would say, "I can hear the running water!" It was amazing.

The listening friend got very sick and eventually died. The first friend cut his harp strings and stopped playing forever. Ever since, cutting the harp strings has been a symbol of special friendship.

Louisa just gave me this story for the Handbook. I think she and Zoe are in cahoots. —Annie

Chapter Twenty-Seven

Under certain circumstances there are
few hours in life more agreeable than the hour
dedicated to the ceremony known as afternoon tea.

—HENRY JAMES, *THE PORTRAIT OF A LADY*

The Steeping Leaf was aglow. Small lanterns
dotted the windows and flickering candles
sat high on top of the shelves—safely out
of the grasp of the many children present. Outside on
the patio, I had placed small bouquets of flowers on
each of the tables and put white lights from my parents' Christmas decorations box into the bushes. Even
people strolling by who knew nothing about the party
were coming in to find out what all the excitement
was about. The place was packed, an irony I noted
sadly.

Two reporters from the *Wisconsin State Journal* snapped

pictures, including several shots of kids holding up pink buttons. One came over to me.

"What can you tell me about this Teashop Girls club?"

"It's a friendship club. For girls. There are rules . . . like Teashop Girls don't keep any secrets from each other and never say anything mean on purpose . . ." I stopped. I could feel someone looking at me. Genna had quietly entered the shop and was waiting with an uncertain look on her face. "Would you excuse me for a minute?" I scooted away from the reporter and felt a wave of remorse. I'd been unfair to Genna, and I knew it. Now that she was here, in the Steeping Leaf, I desperately wanted to fix things between us. The shop, I realized, was a building. What had happened *in* the shop, however, didn't have to end. I hoped it wasn't too late.

"Hi, Annie."

"Hi, Genna."

"Listen——"

"No, it's okay. I'm the one who should——"

"I shouldn't have said what I did." She smiled a little.

"I shouldn't have overreacted." We stood looking at each other for a moment, not sure what to do. We both hated sitcoms where people hugged and made up at the end, but there didn't seem like anything else to do.

"I missed you," I said sheepishly. "Hanging out with

my little brothers isn't nearly as fun as reading self-help books with you."

"I missed you, too. I just—when you got the job here, I felt . . . kind of left out." She admitted this in a quiet voice. I was shocked. Genna? Left out? The world revolved around Genna. It always had. What on earth was she talking about? "I mean, you just seemed so grown-up all of a sudden." She waved her arm around, taking the shop in. "It was stupid of me to say we couldn't save the store. We almost did! I'm sorry."

"Genna, I'm the one who is sorry. So, so sorry. I got scared because you and Zo have other friends, and I . . . I've always had just you guys. Which was perfect! I didn't want things to change." I put my hand on her shoulder, still totally disbelieving. It seemed we had both been feeling weird lately. Being our age was not for wimps. We just needed to be more honest with each other.

It had been brave of Genna to come into the shop tonight, and it meant everything to me that even after the way I had acted, she wanted to make things right between us. I was very, very lucky to have a best friend like her.

"I know. I'm scared too. But even if I do make other friends, we're the Teashop Girls. That's like a whole other *word* for friendship. It's on a different level, you know?"

"I do know." I smiled, feeling very relieved. "I'm

sorry I said theater camp was dumb. It'll be awesome. Forgive me?"

"Only if you forgive me, too. I'm just . . . a little lost sometimes, and when I get like that I don't even know what I'm saying."

"Me too." I still couldn't get the surprise out of my voice. We hugged. Zoe clapped solemnly. We pulled her over and made it a group hug.

"I'm so glad I didn't have to beat anyone with my racket to get this figured out," Zoe said. "I totally would've, too."

"I know," I said seriously. "You're the best, Zo." I felt like a weight had been lifted off my shoulders. We hugged again and Genna got buttons for us. We gathered all the girls in the shop for a solemn reading of the Teashop Girls rules and to ceremoniously pass around the Handbook. The new members were jumping around with excitement. Unfortunately, I just couldn't shake my melancholy about the fate of the Leaf. Even seeing little Hieu with his mom wasn't enough to make me forget about it.

Luckily, Genna and Zo were sticking close to me and it made me feel a lot better. Zoe's mom and stepdad came over just then.

"Zoe, it is getting late," her mom said. "It's been a lovely party, Annie, but I'm afraid we need to go."

"It's only 8:30," Zoe said. I was surprised she was so calm. I frowned.

"You'll have several important exams next week," her stepdad said.

"But it is a Saturday, and I've already studied a lot to prepare. I know you guys just want me to do well, but I learned from Louisa, that everyone needs balance. Time with my friends is important to me."

Genna and I looked at Zoe in surprise. She never, ever stood up to her parents. Zoe met their eyes levelly. They looked at each other and nodded.

"All right, dear." Zoe's mom said. "I suppose that is reasonable. You may stay until the end of the party, but please come right home then."

"I will. Thank you." Zoe let out a breath as her parents wandered away. I turned to her in amazement.

"Zoe, that was incredible. I can't believe they changed their minds."

"I know! Me either. I've been practicing meditation a lot lately, and it's actually made dealing with them much easier." Zoe stood up a little straighter and grinned.

"Wow," Genna said, admiringly.

"They only want what's best," Zoe added, "So I just have to show them, sometimes, that I need my own time."

Mr. Silverman found me and we clinked our cups, his full of oolong and mine full of chai. He didn't have a book today, but he did have a broad grin on his face.

"I hear from your grandmother that you did most of the work putting this party together, Miss Annie. Lovely job. Your grandfather would've been very proud of you."

"Oh, Louisa did her fair share as well, Mr. Silverman. She's got more energy than I do!" I corrected.

"Thirty years . . . imagine. When this place opened, I could touch my toes." He looked around, taking it all in. I shook my head in disbelief. Thirty years was indeed a very long time. I thanked Mr. Silverman for coming.

The party continued at full steam. Louisa put on some jazz and some of the older people taught the teenagers how to jitterbug. The extra chairs got folded up and stored away. Everyone laughed and the little kids jumped up and down. They were naturals. Louisa came up to Mr. Silverman and me. He bowed with a smile and wandered off to find his wife.

"Look at the little girls." We turned around to see a trio of six-year-olds carefully pouring tea for someone's dad. "Aren't they adorable?" I asked.

"They are. Little angels, all of them."

"They want to be Teashop Girls. Just like us when we were that age."

"They sure do. And since you're taking new members . . ."
Louisa proudly displayed her own pink button. "Count me in."

"You can be Tea Empress for Life."

"It's a deal. Now, you have to tell me why you never introduced me to that distinguished gentleman in the corner before. We've been having the most lovely chat."

"Mr. Arun? Oh, that's my school principal. I invited him because he was sort of nice about us handing out samples in the cafeteria. Peach ginger is his favorite tea."

"He's quite handsome. And I do think we'll be seeing more of each other." I looked at my grandmother in shock. I realized that Louisa and Mr. Arun were probably about the same age. I blushed. It was *so* embarrassing to think about old people acting all swoony. Thank goodness, however, Louisa hadn't mentioned any retirement villas in different countries lately. Perhaps a little romance would keep her in Madison forever.

"Seeing more of each other?"

"Yes, indeed," she said with a mischievous grin. "I just wanted to say that I really appreciate all your hard work, dear. Thank you for everything you've done."

"I wish I could've done more. So much more."

"About that," Louisa said with a twinkle in her eye. "I have an announcement to make. Can you get everyone's attention?"

"Um, sure." I looked at Louisa uncertainly. *What now?* It seemed like it was time for the final farewell, and my heart was heavy. I stopped the music and stepped up to the microphone. I thanked everyone for coming and introduced Louisa.

My grandmother stepped up to the microphone. She had a big smile on her face and a cup in her hand.

"Thank you for being here, everyone. What a beautiful evening to come together as friends and neighbors. Thanks again." She paused. "Some of you may have heard about the Steeping Leaf's struggles of late. I'm afraid I'm not the savviest businesswoman, though hiring Annie here was certainly a good move." She paused, and I smiled shyly as everyone's head swiveled in my direction. "Anyway, I recently made the decision to close the shop, fearing that I could not meet our rent obligations."

The crowd gasped. Clearly, not everyone had heard the sad news. Some people started talking excitedly in protest. Louisa silenced them by raising her hand.

"Wait. Like I said, I planned to close the Steeping Leaf after thirty years of business. But tonight, all that changed. I was introduced to two lovely people, Mr. and Mrs. Anderson, developers here in Madison. The Andersons heard about the Steeping Leaf from their son Zach, who is a classmate of my lovely granddaughter." I gasped as people looked at me again. Louisa gestured to the couple, who I just now noticed were standing near the counter with, of course, their nefarious son. Zach was inching away from them, no doubt to cause trouble. *What were they doing here?* "Out of a spirit of generosity and nostalgia, the Andersons have decided to do something to help us. They've contacted the current property owner and arranged to buy this building." I looked at Genna and Zoe, who were as puzzled as I was. "I've just been informed that they would both like our shop to stay in business . . . and have decided to generously stabilize our rent. The Steeping Leaf will stay open!"

The shop erupted in cheers. Mr. and Mrs. Anderson looked embarrassed as various people hugged them. I ran to Louisa and threw my arms around her. I spilled my tea, but I didn't care.

"I can't believe it! This is totally incredible."

"I know, Annie. It *is* incredible. And something tells me that all these new little Teashop Girls are going to keep us *very* busy. Mr. and Mrs. Anderson are now part owners of the business and I think they'll both be very happy with their investment."

I wandered away from Louisa, head in a daze.

"So now that I'm your new boss, Green, I expect you to smarten up. I'm thinking a hairnet for sure." Zach stood in my path, looking pleased with himself. I just stuck out my tongue at him and started grinning. I couldn't help it!

I rushed over to Gen and Zo to have an official freak-out. We were all too happy about the shop, however, to care very much about Zach. Even if his parents were condo royalty, they recognized the things that would make their developments successful were Madison treasures like the Leaf. *Thank goodness.*

"You did it! You saved the shop." Genna was practically bouncing. "If you hadn't started working here, Annie, the Andersons never would've heard of the store because Zach never would've tried the tea or come in here to bother you!" I thought about it. It was a good day. I beamed.

Zoe and I went outside for a little bit to calm down and look in at the scene. We were giddy from the dancing and so very happy about our shop.

"So, I hate to bring this up, but I noticed Jonathan is here and you didn't even really try to talk to him. Or *about* him," Zoe said.

"Yeah. I sort of just realized the other day we don't really have that much in common. I mean, he's still completely gorgeous and everything, but maybe not, like, my One True Love."

My rowdy family arrived at the Steeping Leaf at that moment.

"Are we too late?" my dad asked. "I wore a special shirt!" It said, "Milk and Sugar are for Wimps." My mom squeezed my arm and wandered off to find Louisa. The boys got busy looking for things to spill, and Beth immediately found a table where she could sit and look cool.

"Thanks for coming, Dad. Did you hear the good news?"

"High tea" in England was served late in the day and had hearty dinner foods. It was traditionally served on the main, or high, table of the house to workers who had certainly missed the earlier teatime. Afternoon tea, or "low tea," was usually served around four o'clock in a sitting room or parlor. These sitting rooms had low tables (like coffee tables today). A full afternoon tea featured savories such as little sandwiches as well as scones with jam and cream and sweets served on china. Today we call this sort of meal "high tea," even though this is technically not correct. It sounds so nice, though, don't you agree?

Chapter Twenty-Eight

May you always have walls for the winds, a roof for the
rains, tea beside the fire, laughter to cheer you, those you
love near you, and all your heart might desire.

—AN IRISH BLESSING

Annie Green's Reasons
Why Life Is Beautiful

1. Made up with Genna. Yay. She's taking me to
   Samadhi Spa with her mom before she leaves for
   camp. Woo-hoo! (Didn't make up with her so
   she'd take me to the spa. The two are unrelated.
   Really.)

2. Made more Teashop Girls buttons and special
   cups for the little girls who came into the Leaf
   and now it is a full-fledged craze. We had
   pink T-shirts printed and everything. They
   have a picture of a teacup with a leaf inside

and the Ten Rules of Teashop Girlhood on the back. They treat me like I am a real-life movie star or something. Could def get used to all the adoration.

3. Business at the Steeping Leaf is excellent. Louisa says she's never sold so much rooibos in her life. She's even sold some of Genna's drawings, too!

4. It's summer! Double YES! This means I get to spend all of my time at either the Leaf or in the lake or at the Memorial Union terrace, my second favorite spot on earth! I am going to be so tan by fall. Well, maybe at least my freckles could, like, connect.

The day before the last day of school, I went into the Steeping Leaf on my day off. I found a table on the patio with three empty chairs and claimed it. Louisa was behind the counter, talking animatedly on the phone to, as she now said, "Davishoney," like it was one word. I tried not to think about the fact that Louisa was being all lovey-dovey with my *principal* . . . but then I wondered if maybe improving my principal's love life would improve my own grades. I mean, don't all principals know each other? Surely Mr. Arun could put in a good word for me at Madison West. It was worth looking into.

To set a good Teashop Girls example, I had decided that we were going to start following all the rules again. From now on, Wednesdays meant teatime.

Genna arrived. She was leaving for camp in two days, but promised she would always be around for the Teashop Girls first and foremost the second she got back. Her mom was limiting her theater tryouts to *local* shows and productions, so I knew I wouldn't have to share my best friend with Hollywood . . . yet.

Next, Zoe rolled up on her bike. For once, her tennis racket was not on her back. Her shiny hair was loose, falling in her face. I poured her a cup of healthy green tea and dug out our Handbook. It was definitely time for some new entries.

Louisa brought a fresh pot of tea and a stacked tower of three plates full of goodies. There were little cakes and mini sandwiches. On top were three petit fours, one for each founding Teashop Girl. We dug in. At the next table over, three younger girls were doing the same.

It seemed there were Teashop Girls just about every-where, friends who would see me through anything, whether it was finally giving up on a hopeless crush or saving a special place so other people could discover it. It was summer, and I knew it would be a great one.